The air was suddenly scalding hot.

"I'm sorry," Shaw finally said.

"Don't," Sabrina snapped.

"I shouldn't have left you alone in there."

"You have to learn to put this baby first," Sabrina said. "You can't use how you feel about me as an excuse not to love this child."

"You're wrong. I love this baby." He paused. "And you have no idea how I feel about you."

Sabrina was about to challenge him, but before she could even catch her breath, his mouth went to hers. He was gentle. The kiss, clever. With just the right amount of pressure to please her, and make her want more.

DELORES FOSSEN

THE BABY'S GUARDIAN

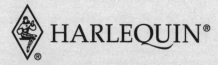

HARLEQUIN®

TORONTO • NEW YORK • LONDON
AMSTERDAM • PARIS • SYDNEY • HAMBURG
STOCKHOLM • ATHENS • TOKYO • MILAN • MADRID
PRAGUE • WARSAW • BUDAPEST • AUCKLAND

Recycling programs for this product may not exist in your area.

ISBN-13: 978-0-373-74526-5

THE BABY'S GUARDIAN

Copyright © 2010 by Delores Fossen

This edition published by arrangement with Harlequin Books S.A.

For questions and comments about the quality of this book please contact us at Customer_eCare@Harlequin.ca.

www.eHarlequin.com

Printed in U.S.A.

ABOUT THE AUTHOR

Imagine a family tree that includes Texas cowboys, Choctaw and Cherokee Indians, a Louisiana pirate and a Scottish rebel who battled side by side with William Wallace. With ancestors like that, it's easy to understand why Texas author and former air force captain Delores Fossen feels as if she was genetically predisposed to writing romances. Along the way to fulfilling her DNA destiny, Delores married an air force top gun who just happens to be of Viking descent. With all those romantic bases covered, she doesn't have to look too far for inspiration.

Books by Delores Fossen

Don't miss any of our special offers. Write to us at the following address for information on our newest releases.

Harlequin Reader Service
U.S.: 3010 Walden Ave., P.O. Box 1325, Buffalo, NY 14269
Canadian: P.O. Box 609, Fort Erie, Ont. L2A 5X3

CAST OF CHARACTERS

Captain Shaw Tolbert—This Texas top cop is at odds with Sabrina Carr, the surrogate carrying his child, because he partly blames her for his late wife's death. What he hadn't counted on was having to fight the attraction he feels for his baby's mother.

Sabrina Carr—She made a promise to Shaw's dying wife to take care of him, and that's the reason Sabrina decided to be his surrogate.

Gavin Cunningham—A young and upcoming attorney who asked Sabrina to help him locate his birth father, but Gavin could have more than a father and son reunion on his mind.

Detective Keith Newell—He's a San Antonio cop close to the maternity hostage investigation. Maybe too close?

Wilson Rouse—This wealthy, outspoken businessman is drawn into the investigation because of a connection to one of the suspects.

Danny Monroe—A computer tech. He's either an innocent pawn or one of the masterminds behind the hostage incident.

Lt. Bo Duggan—Shaw's right-hand man whose wife died during the hostage standoff. Now, Bo's not just the widowed father of twins, he's a key part of the investigation.

Dr. Claire Nicholson—Sabrina's doctor. She had access to Sabrina's medical records, and it's possible someone used information from those records to help set up the hostage situation.

Chapter One

The sound of the gunshot sent Captain Shaw Tolbert's heart to his knees.

Hell. This couldn't happen. He couldn't lose a single one of those hostages.

"Hold your fire!" Shaw shouted to the nearly three dozen officers and SWAT team members he had positioned all around the San Antonio Maternity Hospital.

For a split second everything and everyone around him froze. No more frantic orders and chatter from his men. Even the reporters and photographers who were pressed against the barricades nearly a block away went still, their cameras no longer flashing the bursts of light that knifed through the night.

The stunned silence didn't last. The officers and the SWAT team already had their weapons ready, and they adjusted, taking aim in the direction of that shot.

But the shot hadn't come from any of them.

It'd come from the fourth floor where a group of pregnant women, newborns and hospital staff were all being held at gunpoint. Hostages that included Nadine Duggan, the wife of one of Shaw's own men, Lieutenant Bo Duggan.

That shot meant Nadine or one of the others could have been killed.

Shaw didn't know all the hostages' names. Heck, he wasn't even sure he had an accurate head count. Basically, anyone unlucky enough to have been on the fourth floor at 3:00 p.m. had been taken captive by at least two gunmen wearing ski masks and carrying assault weapons. Shaw had managed to get that meager bit of information from a nurse who'd made a hysterical nine-one-one call during the first minutes of the attack. Since then, neither the nurse nor any of the other known hostages had answered their cells or the hospital phones.

Using the back of his hand to swipe the slick sweat from his forehead, Shaw maneuvered his way through his men and the equipment and hurried from his command center vehicle to the hostage negotiator. It was Texas hot, and the unforgiving August heat was still brutal despite the sun having set hours earlier.

He spotted the negotiator, Sergeant Harris McCoy, in the passenger seat of a patrol car that several officers were using as cover. The blond-haired, blue-eyed officer might look as if he'd just stepped off a glossy recruitment poster, but he was the best that San Antonio PD had. In the past four years, Harris had successfully negotiated nearly twenty hostage situations. Shaw desperately needed him to add one more gold star to his résumé.

"What happened?" Shaw asked.

Harris shook his head. "I'm not sure. I was talking to one of the gunmen on his cell— trying to get the guy to give us his demands. Then he shouted 'she's getting away' and he hung up. About five seconds later, someone fired the shot."

Shaw cursed. He prayed that shot had been fired as a warning and not deadly force. Because if a hostage had been killed, he'd have to seriously consider storming the place ASAP. He couldn't sit back and let all those people die. But the SWAT team and police forcing their way onto the ward would almost certainly cause its own set of casualties.

"Try to get one of the gunmen back on the line," Shaw told Harris.

While Harris pressed redial and waited for the gunman to answer, Shaw held his breath and paced. Not that he could go far. The scene was a logjam of law enforcement officers who'd initially responded, and more had arrived as this ordeal had dragged on. Nine hours. God knew what kind of havoc the gunmen could have created in that much time.

"What happened?" Harris demanded the moment he had one of the gunmen on the phone. Like the other calls throughout the afternoon and evening, this one was on speaker.

"Everything's under control," the gunman assured him. Which was no assurance at all.

After nine hours, Shaw was familiar with that voice, though the guy had refused to identify himself. But it was a voice Shaw would remember, and when he had everyone safely out of this, he was going after this SOB and his accomplice. That wasn't his normal role as a captain. These days, he was pretty much a supervisor working from his desk, but for this, he'd make an exception and do some field duty.

"Is anyone hurt?" Harris asked the gunman.

"No. It was a misunderstanding, that's all. It won't happen again. Will it?"

"No," someone said. A woman. And her voice created an uneasy feeling inside Shaw.

No way.

It couldn't be *her*.

Shaw jerked his phone from his pocket and scrolled through the numbers until he found Sabrina Carr's. He jabbed the call button. Waited. And cursed when he heard the ringing. Not just on his own phone, but the sound was also coming through Harris's cell. Each ring went unanswered, and each ring confirmed that this nightmare had just gotten a lot worse. Sabrina's phone was on the fourth floor of that hospital.

And so was she.

"That was Sabrina Carr's voice," Shaw managed to say to Harris in a whisper.

Harris's head whipped up, and he pinned his alarmed gaze to Shaw's. "You mean…" Harris mouthed, but he didn't finish.

Shaw didn't finish it for him, either, but they both knew what this meant. Sabrina Carr was the surrogate carrying Shaw's child. She was eight months pregnant.

And Sabrina was a hostage.

Shaw resisted the urge to lean against the

patrol car that was just inches away, and he choked back the profanity. This was a complication he didn't need, and the situation had just gotten a lot more personal.

"Are you certain the hostage is all right?" Harris demanded from the gunman.

"See for yourself," the man answered.

Shaw looked up at the row of eight-foot-tall windows that encircled the entire fourth floor. The building was about thirty yards away, but he still saw the movement behind the thick glass.

Someone pushed a woman into view.

The height and build were right for it to be Sabrina. About five-six and average. So was the pregnant belly that her tan cargo shorts and bulky green top couldn't hide. Ditto for that mop of shoulder-length red hair—Sabrina had hair like that. But praying he was wrong, Shaw grabbed a pair of binoculars from the officer next to him and took a closer look.

Hell.

It was Sabrina all right.

She was shades past being pale, and he could tell from her expression that she was terrified. Probably because she'd just come close to dying. That shot had no doubt been fired at her.

Even though there was no love lost between

Sabrina and him, Shaw wasn't immune to the terror he saw on her face and in her eyes. After all, she was carrying his child.

Their child, he silently amended.

The image of his late wife flashed through his head. The baby Sabrina was carrying should have been his wife's. His and Fay's. Sabrina should have been just a surrogate, that's all, but that had changed when none of Fay's eggs had been viable. Sabrina had become the egg donor then, too. Sabrina's DNA, not Fay's. More than a mere surrogate. But that was an old wound that he didn't have time to nurse right now.

"Did you know Sabrina was in there?" Harris asked, placing his hand over the receiver so the gunman wouldn't be able to hear the question.

Shaw shook his head. Sabrina had her regular prenatal checkups at a clinic in the hospital, but she wasn't scheduled for anything this week. Shaw knew that because she always sent him the dates and times of her appointments. Not that he'd ever gone with her to any of them. But he knew she wasn't scheduled for anything until the day after tomorrow.

So, why was she there?

"Ask to speak to her," Shaw instructed.

Harris nodded. "I want to talk to the hostage

to make sure she's okay," he relayed to the gunman.

The gunman didn't respond right away, and with the binoculars pressed to his eyes, Shaw watched. Waited.

The seconds crawled by.

Then, much to his surprise, he saw the gloved hand jut out and give Sabrina the cell phone.

Because Shaw was watching her so closely, he saw her look in the direction of that hand. The gunman's hand. Shaw could hear the man give her whispered instructions, but he couldn't make out what the guy was saying. It was almost certainly some kind of threat.

"Captain Shaw Tolbert?" she said.

That sent another hush around him. Inside, Shaw was having a much stronger reaction than a hush. Why the devil was she asking for him? If the gunmen knew her association with the captain of the SAPD, things could get even worse for her.

And the baby.

"Yes?" Shaw answered, trying to sound official and detached. Judging from the sound of her voice, the call was on speaker at Sabrina's end, which meant the gunmen were listening to his every word. He certainly didn't want to let them know that he knew her name, just in case he could salvage this situation.

"They read my medical records," Sabrina explained. She swallowed hard. "They know you're my emergency contact."

Shaw choked back a groan. By knowing that bit of information, the gunmen had already guessed that Sabrina and he had some kind of relationship. Heck, her records might even say that he was the baby's father. If so, the gunmen had some serious leverage.

Both Sabrina and the baby.

"Are you…all right?" Shaw asked.

"She is, for now," the gunman answered for her. "You'll need to do some things to make it stay that way."

Even though he could clearly hear the man, Shaw took Harris's phone and brought it closer to his mouth. "What things?"

The gunman grabbed Sabrina's phone as well, but she stayed in the window, staring down at the crowd. He saw her pick through the faces until she spotted him. Shaw looked away. He needed to focus, and he couldn't do that if he was looking at her. Because looking at Sabrina only brought on those haunting images of his wife.

A man didn't forget watching his wife die in his arms.

"My partner and I are ready to get out of here," the gunman announced.

Shaw didn't celebrate either silently or aloud because he knew this was just the first step to ending this, and every step afterward would be even more dangerous than the present situation.

"We're coming out through the front entrance," the gunman continued. "And we'll have a hostage with us."

They were probably planning to take Sabrina, unless Shaw could get them to change their minds.

"So, no tricks," the gunman warned. "Have your officers back way off and have a car waiting for us out front. We'll give the driver instructions as to where we need to go."

Shaw sandwiched the phone between his shoulder and his ear so he could motion for one of his men to spring into action. They'd anticipated the car request and had one ready. A vehicle with not one but two hidden GPS trackers that would allow them to find the guys.

Well, maybe.

There was something not quite right about all of this.

The gunmen hadn't requested money or any other form of ransom. That wasn't just unusual, it was downright unsettling. After all, the men had just spent hours holding the hostages, and they'd done that without saying why this situation had started in the first place. A hospital maternity ward wasn't the setting for many hostage standoffs, especially since this didn't seem to be personal.

At least it hadn't been until now.

Had the gunmen gone after Sabrina in the first place, or had that happened only after they'd learned about her connection to an SAPD police captain? Maybe the plan was to take her to a secondary location and ask for ransom?

That theory would have held some merit if Shaw had been a rich man. He wasn't.

So, what did the men want?

Drugs, maybe. That was always a possibility when it came to hospital robberies. Maybe that was all there was to it. They'd wanted drugs and now they had them and needed to get away. That didn't lessen the danger, but it would make the investigation a little simpler.

The officer parked the car in front of the hospital, and Shaw motioned for everyone to move away. He would pull all his men back onto the sidewalk of the building across the four lanes of St. Mary's Street. The SWAT team would stay in place on the rooftops. Because the surrounding buildings were taller than the hospital, Shaw didn't think the gunmen had actually seen the SWAT team. But still, they must have known they were there. This hostage situation was all over the news, and the world was watching. The gunmen must have realized that every conceivable measure would have been taken to apprehend them.

"The car's in place," Shaw told the gunman over the cell.

"Good. We're coming out. Remember, no tricks."

"My advice? Don't take one of the new mothers or pregnant women hostage. Too much trouble, and too many things can go wrong. Take me instead."

"No, thanks. I got my own ideas about how to handle a hostage." And the gunman hung up.

Shaw didn't have time to react to that bold threat because movement caught his eye. A gloved hand reached out and grabbed on to Sabrina's arms. She snagged Shaw's gaze then. For just a second. And the gunman yanked her out of sight.

It sickened Shaw to think of the stress this was creating for the baby. And the danger. No unborn child or pregnant woman should have to go through this, and Shaw had to make sure this ended now.

Shaw relayed the information he'd just learned to one of the uniforms who would pass it on to the other officers posted at various points around the building. He handed the phone back to Harris, and he drew his gun while he moved back across the street with his men. He kept his attention fastened to the front of the building. Watching. Bracing himself for whatever was about to go down.

When the gunmen came out, it was possible the SWAT team would have clean shots, but if that didn't happen, the plan was to let the gunmen drive away and have plainclothes officers in unmarked cars follow in pursuit. Then, he could get his men inside the building to assess the damage. It was entirely possible they would have dead bodies or injuries on their hands. Ambulances were waiting just up the street since the hospital itself had already been evacuated, and the staff inside might need medical attention of their own.

Shaw wouldn't be able to hold back the lieutenant whose wife was inside, so he hoped this departure ended with the gunmen being killed.

If not, well, the night was just starting.

"Smoke!" Harris shouted.

Shaw looked in the direction of Harris's pointing finger. Oh, mercy.

What now?

It was smoke all right, and it was coming from a window on the fourth floor where the hostages were.

There was a fire engine standing by, and Shaw motioned for it to get in place. It was a huge risk. The gunmen might not come down to the car if they saw the fire department responding, but Shaw couldn't take the chance of leaving those hostages trapped on the floor with a raging fire.

"The hospital has an overhead sprinkler system," Harris reminded him.

But no one needed to remind Shaw that the gunmen could have disabled it. God knows what smoke and fire would do to all those babies in the newborn unit. He had to get them help immediately, even if it meant the gunmen might get away.

"Where are they?" Shaw mumbled, watching the front door.

The fire engine darted across the street and stopped at the side of the building. They immediately retrieved the ladder so they could scurry up the four floors. It was a start, but Shaw needed to get others inside so he could speed up the evacuation. In addition to the babies, there might be patients who couldn't get out on their own.

The passing seconds pounded in his head, and at least a minute went by with no sign of the gunmen or the hostage that they claimed they would have with them.

Gray coils of smoke made their way down to them. Soon, very soon, it would obstruct their view. And maybe that's what the gunmen had intended.

Shaw grabbed the binoculars again and checked out the front windows on the fourth floor. He could see the overhead sprinklers spewing out water. He could also see people running. Women. Some of them pregnant. Some of them carrying babies bundled in blankets.

He couldn't delay this any longer. He had to move now.

Shaw was about to give the signal when he heard the voice on the hand-sized scanner clipped to his belt. It was Lieutenant Bo Duggan, the officer who was positioned on the west side of the building.

"The fire's a smokescreen!" Bo shouted. "The gunmen just left through the side door and got into a white SUV with heavy tint on the windows. I can't see the license plate number—it had mud or something covering it—and they're moving out of the parking lot now."

Hell.

"Shaw?" Bo said. "We couldn't shoot at them because they have a hostage. It's Sabrina Carr."

Shaw's stomach knotted, but he forced back the avalanche of emotion and dread. "Take over the evacuation," he ordered Bo. "Get everyone out of there." He turned to Harris. "You get in there, too. Take every available man." Shaw turned to run toward his squad car.

"Where are you going?" Harris shouted.

"After the gunmen."

And every second counted.

Shaw had already lost his wife, and by God he wasn't going to let the same thing happen to his baby.

Chapter Two

Sabrina forced herself to stay calm.

It was nearly impossible to do that because there was a gun jammed against her head, and one of the ski-mask-wearing kidnappers shoved her into the backseat of an SUV. The other got behind the wheel and sped out of the parking lot.

There were plenty of officers nearby, all with guns aimed, but none of them fired a shot. Probably because they hadn't wanted to risk wounding her and the baby. Sabrina was thankful for that, but she wondered if she'd just gone from the frying pan into the fire.

Her heart was racing, and it was so loud in her ears that it was hard for her to hear, but she thought she might have heard one of the officers shout. Maybe that meant someone would follow them because she wasn't sure she'd be able to get herself out of this without help.

She glanced behind her at the hospital. The building was engulfed in milky gray smoke, but she could still see even more cops. Some armed with rifles were on top of the surrounding buildings.

Shaw was out there, too.

Sabrina had seen him from the window. He'd been standing among all the officers assembled to respond to the hostage situation. And even though Shaw had been so far away when she stepped into view, she had been able to make out his expression when he realized she was a hostage. That wasn't fear on his face. More like anger.

Or even disgust.

He was probably thinking she'd screwed up again.

And in a way, she had.

The gunman-driver made a sharp left turn and sent her sliding toward the door. Her captor hauled her right back so he could keep her in a close, firm grip against his side. She wanted to punch him for what he was doing.

For what he'd done back at the hospital.

Sabrina had seen him shoot an unarmed lab tech who was hardly more than a kid. He'd used a gun rigged with a silencer for that deadly assault, and the shot had hardly made a sound. It made her wonder how many others had been killed in a silent hush.

And why?

Why would be the biggest question of all.

Was it connected to the call from the nurse, Michael Frost, that she'd gotten earlier? The call that sent her to the hospital in the first place?

Maybe.

But for now, her focus had to be on survival. The cops were no doubt following them, and she had to believe they would launch a rescue. She also had to believe they would succeed. Sabrina couldn't even consider an alterative, not with her baby's safety at stake.

She looked up at the street signs, trying to memorize them just in case she got the opportunity to tell someone where she was, but the gunman must have noticed what she was doing because he shoved her down onto the seat.

"Curiosity killed the cat," he snarled. He stank of sweat, onion chips from the hospital vending machine and the peppermint breath mints that he'd sucked on throughout the standoff.

Sabrina would remember that sickening scent. That raspy voice. Those dull brown eyes that were flat, like a man on the job rather than one on a personal mission.

He was almost certainly a hired killer.

And when this was over, she would make sure he and his partner were punished for this havoc they had caused. All those women and babies had been put through a nightmare, and it wasn't over. Not for her, not for them. They would have to deal with the terrifying memories forever.

Something that Sabrina already knew too much about.

"We lost the cops," the driver announced.

That didn't help with the fear or the dread. But he could be wrong. *He had to be wrong*.

The driver slowed to a crawl, and several seconds later, the car came to a stop. In a dark alley.

Oh, God.

Sabrina tried not to think of what could happen here. She didn't think these men had rape or assault on their minds, but they wouldn't hesitate to use her as a human shield when the cops arrived.

"Move fast," the gunman ordered, and he threw open the door and pushed her out into the alley.

"Right," she grumbled. Fast wasn't possible for her these days.

She didn't see any other cars or people. Definitely no cops. And her heartbeat grew significantly harder and faster. God. Had the driver been right about SAPD not being able to follow her? Had the gunmen made a clean getaway?

The gunman latched on to her arm and dragged her into the adjacent building. It was dark, musky and hot. No AC. Not even a trickle of fresh air. No furniture, either. From what Sabrina could see in the shadows, it was an abandoned office building, and judging from the distance they'd driven, they were somewhere in the downtown area of San Antonio. Not a good part, either.

"Lock the door," the gunman told his partner. "I'll tie her up. But don't make the call until you're out of her earshot. No sense broadcasting what's going on."

The man didn't take her to a room near the door but to one about midway down the long tiled corridor. He shoved his gun into the back waist of his pants so he could use both hands to snag her wrists.

Sabrina knew what was coming.

She'd already seen him tie up members of the hospital staff and some of the patients. He took two thin plastic handcuffs from his pocket and looped one around her wrists. The other, he hooked through the first so that it chained her to the doorknob. The plastic cuffs might be cheap, but they were extremely effective. They would hold her in place until…but Sabrina didn't want to think beyond that.

She would get out of this before they managed to take her out of the city and to God knows where.

She needed a miracle.

The man reached down and pulled off her sandals. "In case you figure out how to get out of those cuffs, there's broken glass on the floor. It'll slice your feet to shreds," he snarled and went down the hall with her shoes dangling in his hand.

Being shoeless wouldn't stop her, either. Sabrina looked around the dark room, praying there was something she could use to cut the tough plastic. Maybe a piece of the glass he'd mentioned. It was there, all right. Beer bottles had been shattered, but none of the pieces was close enough for her to reach.

There were only threads of light coming from the single window on the center wall. The glass panes were coated with grime and taped yellowing newspapers that practically blocked off illumination from the nearby streetlights. But it allowed her to see just enough to realize there was nothing she could use as a cutter. With the exception of the broken glass and some trash on the floor, the room was empty.

Inside her, the baby began to kick, hard. Probably to protest her cramped sitting position. Sabrina shifted, trying to get more comfortable, but that was impossible on a hard tile floor.

Up the hall, she heard the peppermint-popping gunman say something, and she wiggled closer to the doorway in the hopes that she could hear and see what was going on. The men had apparently stepped into one of the other rooms because they were nowhere in sight, but she did get bits and pieces of their softly spoken conversation.

"Tolbert," one of them said.

That grabbed her attention. They were talking about Shaw. Sabrina tried to wriggle even closer though the plastic cuffs were digging into her wrists.

"It'll work." That was from the gunman who'd driven them away from the hospital. He was whispering as if he wanted to ensure she didn't hear what he was saying, but the empty building carried the sound. "We can use her to get Tolbert to cooperate in case something else turns up."

Oh, God. They were going to use her to

force Shaw to do something. But cooperate with what?

All of this had to be connected to the hostage mess that'd just gone on in the hospital, but Sabrina was clueless as to why she and the others had been terrorized all those hours.

What did any of this have to do with Shaw?

The men didn't know she was carrying Shaw's child. Or did they? It certainly wasn't in her medical records, but they had seen that she had listed Shaw as the person to contact in case there was an emergency. Maybe the men thought she and Shaw were lovers.

As if.

Shaw hated her with a passion. And this situation was only going to make him hate her more. Once again, she'd brought danger to someone he loved. This time, the danger was aimed at his unborn child. He would never forgive her for placing the baby at risk.

Of course, Sabrina wouldn't forgive herself, either.

Had that call she'd received all been a hoax? Something designed to get her into the hospital?

If so, then her abduction wasn't a spur of the minute thing as she'd originally believed. She might have been their target all along, and she hadn't even questioned the call. She'd blindly responded to the request and had walked right into a hornet's nest.

The minute she'd stepped off that fourth floor elevator, one of the men had aimed a gun at her and then corralled her into the hall where they were already holding several dozen hostages. Sabrina wouldn't forget their faces. The fear. The overwhelming feeling of doom.

"The car'll be here in ten minutes," she heard one of her captors say. "Go ahead, give her back the shoes. I want us to be ready to roll."

Ten minutes. Not much time at all. And judging from their other conversation, they'd be taking her with them. If that happened, they might kill her once they had what they wanted. Because of the ski masks, she hadn't seen their faces, but she did know details about them. She was a loose end and a dangerous one.

The man appeared again, his ski mask still in place, and he carefully placed the shoes on the floor beside her. When she didn't move to slip them on, he cursed at her, shoved them on her feet and walked away.

She waited until he was out of sight before she fought with the plastic cuffs again. No luck. So, she decided to try to chew her way through them, though she knew that would be next to impossible. The cuffs were designed to prevent such an escape. Still, she had to try. Those ten minutes were already ticking off.

There was a sound. Just a slight bump. It didn't come from the men up the hall but from the window.

Someone was outside.

Sabrina chewed even harder on the cuff, while she kept watch up the hall and at the shadowy figure on the other side of that murky glass.

There was a soft pop. And the window eased open. She got a good look at the dark-haired man then.

It was Shaw.

Relief flooded through her entire body. He'd come for her. Well, he'd come for the baby anyway. Now the question was, could he get them safely out of there?

Shaw glanced around the room and put his index finger to his mouth in a stay-quiet gesture. Sabrina quit struggling with the plastic cuffs and tipped her head toward the men up the hall.

"There are two of them," she mouthed, and in case Shaw hadn't heard, she held up two fingers.

Shaw nodded, climbed through the window, swung his legs over the sill and quietly placed his feet on the floor. He had his standard-issue Glock ready in his right hand, and he lifted it, aiming it at the door. If her captors heard Shaw's entrance, they would no doubt come running.

But they didn't.

The men continued to talk, and Shaw used the sound of their muffled voices to cover his footsteps as he made his way across the dusty floor toward her. Shattered glass crunched softly under his feet. He spared her a glance.

Barely.

That was normal. Shaw never looked in her eyes, which was probably a good thing. Even something as simple as eye contact between them brought back the painful memories of Fay's death. But Sabrina knew that his eyes were multiple shades of blue. Cool and piercing when he was in a good mood. Dark and stormy when he was wasn't.

She didn't have to guess the intensity level tonight.

With his attention fastened to the hall and doorway, Shaw reached in his pocket, brought out a small knife and used it to slice through the plastic. He didn't waste a second; he took her arm, got her to her feet and eased her behind him. His hand brushed against her stomach. An accident for sure.

Like eye contact, touching was out, too.

Shaw motioned toward the window. "You think you can climb out?" he whispered.

Sabrina glanced down at her megapregnant belly and then at the window. It'd be a tight squeeze, but the alternative was going out into the hall and then trying to make their way through a locked door at the end. That was far riskier than the window.

She nodded, and he maneuvered her behind him while he continued to face the door.

Shaw leaned closer and put his mouth to her ear. No peppermint and sweat smell for him. She took in the scent of his starched white shirt, the leather of his boots and the woodsy aftershave he favored. Not that he would have shaved recently. He had dark desperado stubble on his chin, but a hint of the aftershave was still there.

"Once we're outside and away from the scene, SWAT will storm the building," Shaw whispered.

Good. This had to end, and she didn't want those gunmen to be able to hurt anyone else.

Thankful that she was wearing shorts so

she could maneuver better, Sabrina somehow managed to get her leg onto the sill. But then, she heard the footsteps in the hall.

Oh, no. One of the gunmen was coming.

Sabrina tried to hurry, but Shaw clamped on to her arm to stop her from moving. Without the sound of her rustling, the room fell silent.

So did the footsteps.

They waited there. Listening. Sabrina prayed the men wouldn't come closer. The last thing she wanted was a gun battle where the baby could be hurt. Obviously, Shaw felt the same because he moved protectively in front of her. Close. With his back right against her front.

As a cop, he'd perhaps been in situations similar to this where his life was on the line, but this whole ordeal was a first for her, and Sabrina hoped she didn't lose it. Falling apart wouldn't get them out of there, and it wouldn't help the baby.

"Call him back," the gunman finally said. It was the peppermint guy. "I'm getting a weird feeling about being here. We need to get out now."

With her breath stalled in her lungs, Sabrina stayed still, and she finally heard what she prayed she would hear. The gunman went back down the hall away from them. At least she hoped that's what he'd done.

Shaw nudged her to get moving, and Sabrina didn't waste any time. She climbed through the window, trying to protect her belly from scraping against the sill. Her feet finally touched down onto the ground. Shaw was right behind her. While continuing to face the direction of the gunmen, he shimmied out the window and landed right next to her.

"Come on," he ordered. Using his left hand, he grabbed her arm and started to move as fast as she could.

The baby kicked even harder, and her stomach started to cramp. Sabrina silently cursed the Braxton Hicks contraction.

False labor.

Her body was merely practicing for the real thing, but she didn't need the distraction now. She had to keep moving and get to safety.

She saw the SWAT team then, on the building across the street. There were other officers crouched down behind a Dumpster and the gunmen's SUV.

The baby and she were safe.

Or so she thought.

But then, the shots rang out.

Chapter Three

Shaw cursed and hooked his arm around Sabrina.

Despite the urgency that the deadly gunfire created, he tried to be careful with her, and he took the brunt of the fall when he pulled her to the ground. His shoulder hit hard, but he held on tight to his gun so that it wouldn't be jarred from his hand.

Shaw didn't stop there. He crawled over Sabrina, sheltering her with his body, and he came up ready to return fire.

This was obviously a situation he'd wanted to avoid at all costs. He didn't want his baby in the middle of a fight with these armed fugitives, but when they fired that shot, they'd left him no choice. Now, the trick was to get Sabrina safely out of there.

There was another shot. It slammed into the rough brick wall just inches from Shaw's head. Not close, a good foot away, but the sound and the impact allowed him to pinpoint the origin of the shot. It was coming from the window where Sabrina and he had escaped.

"Get down," someone on the SWAT team yelled from the roof of the adjacent building.

Shaw did. He dropped lower, covering Sabrina as best he could.

She was breathing way too hard and fast, and he hoped like the devil that she didn't hyperventilate. While he was hoping, he added that the baby hadn't been harmed in all of this. Sabrina didn't appear to have any physical injuries, but the stress couldn't be good. She needed to get to a doctor so she could be checked out.

There was another shot, but this one came from a rifleman on the SWAT team. Shaw didn't look up, but he heard the sound of glass being blown apart.

Good!

That would stop the gunmen from aiming any more shots at Sabrina and him. At least from that window. That didn't mean they wouldn't go elsewhere to return fire. The abandoned building was large, at least five thousand square feet, and there were a lot of places for someone to hide or get into a position to kill.

The shots continued, all coming from his men, which meant it might be time to try to get Sabrina to better cover. Shaw glanced at the front of the building. Hell.

Too many windows.

And a set of double doors with glass fronts.

The gunmen could use any of those points of attack to fire again. That meant staying put until the officers and SWAT had apprehended the suspects. The one advantage that his officers did have was that the building was only one floor. The gunmen wouldn't be able to move upstairs and launch an assault there. They were going to have to face the SWAT team and other cops head-on.

So that Sabrina's pregnant belly wouldn't be smashed against the ground, Shaw eased off her and moved her to a sitting position so that her back was against the brick wall. They were close. Too close. And face-to-face.

He found himself staring right into those sea-green eyes.

Shaw quickly looked away. Then he turned around so he was facing outward. This would make it easier for him to cover all sides. It was a solid strategic move, he assured himself. And it was far better than staring at her.

With the gunmen no longer firing at them,

Shaw's men started to close in around the building. One of the SWAT members bashed in the double front doors, and officers began to pour inside. It shouldn't be long now before he could get Sabrina out of there.

Once he had her in an ambulance and on the way to a hospital, he could return to the original crime scene and try to mop up things. He'd left Lieutenant Bo Duggan in charge, but that was strictly temporary. Since Bo's own wife was a hostage, Shaw needed to get back on scene so that Bo could be with his wife. If their situations had been reversed, Shaw would have certainly wanted to be with Fay.

"The gunmen said they were going to use me," Sabrina muttered, her voice a shaky whisper. But it was loud enough to cut through his thoughts and snare his attention. "To get *you* to cooperate."

"What?" Shaw said that a little louder than he'd intended and glanced at her over his shoulder.

Sabrina shook her head, sending a curl of that wild red hair flinging over her cheek. "I don't know what they meant by that. Do you?"

"No." But he could guess. "I'm a police captain." A lot of people might want him to *cooperate,* especially when it came to helping with a plea bargain or reduced charges.

That wouldn't happen in this case.

Shaw turned his head away from her so he could keep watch of all the areas around them. "What else did they say?"

"Not much. They were careful not to talk in front of me or the others. But I think they knew I'd be at the hospital this afternoon. They were waiting for me."

Oh, man. That didn't sound good at all. "Why the heck were you even there?"

Sabrina took a deep breath. "Someone from the hospital phoned me. A male nurse named Michael Frost, and he said Nadine Duggan had called an urgent meeting of the moms' support group. So, I went."

Shaw cursed and didn't bother to keep the profanity to himself. Sabrina knew how he felt about that group. It was headed by Nadine Duggan, the wife of one of his lieutenants and a woman who'd also become a hostage. Bo's wife. Nadine was a psychologist and probably bound to keep secret whatever she was told in that support group, but Shaw didn't want Sabrina baring her soul to someone who might share those soul-baring secrets with her husband, a man whom Shaw worked side by side with. Bo and all the other officers knew about Shaw's late wife, of course.

Everyone also knew about the baby.

But Shaw hadn't wanted Sabrina to talk about the problems that he'd had adjusting to her pregnancy. About all the appointments he'd missed for her checkups. All the calls from her that he hadn't returned.

Their arrangement was complicated since, after all, he'd ultimately given her approval to get pregnant. Hell, he'd provided the semen for the procedure, but he and Sabrina both knew he wasn't really on board. Not emotionally.

And it was those emotions Shaw wanted to keep to himself.

Best not to let his men know the mental turmoil he was going through right now. Something like that could perhaps water down his authority, and as their leader, the last thing he wanted in a dangerous situation was to have his authority questioned or undermined.

That's why Shaw had offered to pay for Sabrina to attend another support group. But she'd refused.

What else was new?

They didn't see eye to eye on, well, anything.

"Is that why Nadine Duggan was there at the hospital, too?" Shaw asked, still keeping watch. Another wave of officers went into the building.

"No. She was actually in labor. I saw her when I first arrived, but then she disappeared when the gunmen starting shouting. A lot of people did. It was chaos, and some of the women ran and hid."

Shaw had to take a deep breath. He hoped that didn't mean anything bad had happened to the lieutenant's wife or any of the patients, staff or babies.

"What about this Michael Frost who called you?" he asked. "Did you see him after you arrived at the hospital?"

"No." She paused. "Why?"

"No reason." Not yet anyway. He'd make a call in a minute or two to have a background check run on the male nurse. Everything and everyone would be checked.

"The gunmen killed someone," Sabrina added.

That caused Shaw to glance at her again, and this time those green eyes were filled with tears. "Who?"

"A lab tech. I don't know his name. They shot him. Right in front of me."

This time Shaw added a groan to the pro-fanity. Sabrina had witnessed a murder, and in addition to the emotional trauma that created, it could mean that she was now a target. If those gunmen thought for one minute that she could identify them, they wouldn't want her around, so that's why it was critical for this to end now.

"Did the men shoot at you, too?" Shaw asked.

She didn't answer right away. "Yes. But not when they killed the tech. It was later. I could tell they were getting ready to leave, and I had a gut feeling they'd take me with them. So, I tried to sneak away."

Unfortunately, he could picture that scene all too well.

"The gunman didn't shoot at me, not really," she added. "The bullet went in the ceiling."

Which confirmed the gunmen wanted her alive. After all, the gunmen had already killed others, so that meant they had a reason for allowing Sabrina to live.

Was he that reason?

"I'm sorry, Shaw. I'm so sorry," Sabrina said. But he knew she wasn't talking about this situation alone. She was dredging up the past.

Something he wouldn't discuss with her.

"Don't," he warned.

He didn't add more because his phone buzzed. He glanced at the caller ID and saw it was from the SWAT team commander, Lieutenant José Rivera. "Tolbert," Shaw answered.

"Captain, we need you to stay put for a couple more minutes. We're trying to secure the building now, but we don't want Ms. Carr or you out in the open just yet."

"Yeah. Make it as fast as you can," Shaw insisted. Because he didn't want to stay there with Sabrina any longer than necessary, and he was anxious to get back to the primary crime scene.

Shaw ended the call and waited with the sounds of the search going on in the building behind them. He didn't stop watching the place. Definitely didn't lower his gun. Because he didn't want those men, those killers, coming back outside to grab Sabrina.

"Think hard," Shaw said. If he had to wait there with her, he might as well start the interrogation that had to happen for the reports and the cleanup. "What did these men want?"

"I don't know."

Sabrina was crying. He could hear the tears in her voice. Part of him wanted to comfort her, but Shaw resisted. He couldn't open up his heart to that kind of intimacy with her. The only way he had survived Fay's death was to shut himself off, and he would continue to do just that.

Shaw tried again with the questions. He wanted to keep this conversation on the business at hand. "Other than you and the lab tech they killed, did it seem as if the gunmen were after anyone specific?"

"They kept calling out for someone named Bailey. I don't think they found her though because they kept shouting her name. And then they had a group of us sit in the hall. One of them held us at gunpoint while the other gunman took this one pregnant woman. I don't know where they took her, but she was gone for several hours. Then, she tried to escape, but she fell and hit her head. She was bleeding."

Each new thing he learned disgusted him even more, and it was just starting. All kinds of details would no doubt be brought out when the other hostages were questioned. He'd definitely need to speak to this woman whom the gunmen had yelled at.

If she was still alive, that is.

"What else did the gunmen do?" he asked. "Did they appear to be searching for anything specific?"

"Other than the person named Bailey, I don't think so." She paused, shook her head.

"Wait. One of them went into the lab and the records room. The lab door wouldn't open so he shot the lock, and he stayed in there a long time. He also had one of the hostages with him a lot of time."

Okay. That was a start. He'd have every inch of those rooms processed and review the surveillance camera footage to see what the men had been after.

"How about a drug cabinet or something like that?" Shaw didn't enjoy forcing her to go over all the details, but with her memory still fresh, this was the time to do it. Later, the shock and the adrenaline crash might rob her of critical details.

"No drugs. At least, I didn't see them take or use any." Behind him, Sabrina shifted her position, probably because she was trying to get comfortable. But with the shift, her belly pressed against his back.

Shaw felt it then.

The soft bumps.

He glanced back at the contact and realized what he was feeling was the baby.

"The baby's kicking," Sabrina explained, moving away again so that she wasn't touching him.

Shaw immediately felt the loss. It was the first time he'd felt his child move. The timing was lousy, but he couldn't totally stop himself from reacting.

In a month, maybe less, he'd be a father.

His phone buzzed again. Thank God. He needed something to slap him back to the moment. It was Rivera, the SWAT team commander.

"Captain, we have a patrol car ready to get you and Ms. Carr out of here. It's pulling up to the curb right now."

Well, that was good news. "And the situation with the search?"

"We have all points of the building secure. But no sign of the gunmen yet. We're still looking."

"Find them!" Shaw ordered after he got his teeth unclenched.

He pulled Sabrina to her feet so he could get her moving. The sooner he had her away from the building, the better.

Even though she was obviously slowed because of the pregnancy, she hurried, keeping up right along with him, but she was breathing hard again by the time he got her into the backseat of the cruiser. The driver, a uniformed officer, drove away.

"Ms. Carr will need to go to a hospital," Shaw instructed the driver.

She didn't protest. Which wasn't a good

sign. Since Sabrina often protested any- and everything he suggested.

Did that mean she was hurt?

While the driver meandered his way through the deserted downtown streets, Shaw called Harris, the hostage negotiator, for a situation report from the maternity hospital. It took a while—four rings—before Harris answered, and the moment Shaw heard the strain in the man's voice, he knew this conversation wasn't going to be good.

"The fire's out," Harris started. "It wasn't much of one. The gunmen lit some damp papers, and that created more smoke than fire."

And they'd used that smoke to escape. "Casualties?" Shaw asked, dreading the answer.

"Four so far."

Shaw cursed. "Not one of the babies?"

"No, they all seem to be fine, but we have doctors on the way to check them all out," Harris answered quickly, and then hesitated. "Three of the dead were on the medical staff here. The other was a patient. She died just a few minutes ago." Another pause. "It was Nadine Duggan."

Ah, hell.

The lieutenant's wife. *A cop's wife.* Shaw had to take a deep breath, but that didn't stop the jolt from the memories of the night his wife had died.

"Nadine was nine months pregnant," Shaw said. He didn't dare look at Sabrina, but he was aware that she was sobbing now. She'd obviously heard what Harris had said. "What happened to her child?"

"They're alive. Twins, a boy and a girl," Harris added in a hoarse whisper. "Bo's taking this pretty hard."

Of course he was. Bo loved his wife, and what was supposed to be one of the happiest days of their lives—the birth of their children—had turned into a nightmare.

"We have another patient clinging to life," Harris continued. "I don't think she's going to make it so we have someone tracking down her next of kin. Another woman is in critical condition. Both of them delivered babies during the standoff."

And this might be just the tip of the iceberg. His men had been in that building less than forty-five minutes. God knew what they would find when they searched every nook and cranny. The death and injury toll might skyrocket.

"Sabrina said some of the women hid," Shaw told Harris. "Some might be too scared to come out. You'll need to look for them."

"Of course. We'll go through the place room by room. How is Sabrina? Did you find her?"

Shaw had to clear his throat before he could speak. "I found her. She's safe." And because he needed to focus on the job, he checked his watch. "I'm dropping her off with a uniformed officer at the hospital on San Pedro, and then I can join you on scene."

"Good. Because we can use all the help we can get."

"Nadine's dead?" Sabrina asked the moment Shaw ended the call.

He settled for a nod.

She pressed her fingers to her mouth, but he still heard the sob. Shaw wasn't sure how well she knew Nadine, but they'd obviously met and chatted in that hospital support group. Plus, Sabrina was no doubt thinking that it could have been her who'd ended up dead.

Shaw was certainly thinking it.

Because Sabrina's sobs were getting louder, he felt he had to do something. Anything. Even if he wasn't sure he wanted to do it.

Shaw slipped his arm around her, and she dropped her head onto his shoulder. He expected the contact to feel foreign and uncomfortable. It did.

It also felt comforting.

She was soft and warm and practically melted against him so Shaw just sat there and let her cry it out. By the time the driver stopped in front of the hospital, he felt raw and drained, and figured that was minor compared to what Sabrina was feeling.

His phone buzzed again, and he flipped it open. Not Harris with reports of more deaths or injuries. This call was from Rivera, the SWAT commander.

"Tell me you have good news," Shaw greeted the man.

But there was only a long heavy moment of silence. "Sorry. We've gone through the abandoned office building, every inch of it, and the gunmen aren't here."

"What?" Shaw snarled. Beside him, Sabrina practically snapped to attention.

"We think they escaped through the basement. We didn't even know there was a basement because there are no marked stairs leading into that area. When we got down there, we found a single small window. Open."

"And no one saw two armed men coming out through that window?"

"No, sir. It was on the south side of the building where there are heavy shrubs, and they might have slipped into those and used them as cover so they could get away."

Hell! This was not supposed to happen. "Those men are killers. We have four DBs on our hands back at the hospital, and two more might soon join the list."

"I understand. These are very dangerous men. We're searching the area now, and I'm bringing in more officers."

"Do that. Do whatever it takes." Shaw slammed his phone shut and cursed.

"They got away," Sabrina mumbled. "They got away." And she continued to repeat it. The more she said it, the closer she sounded to getting hysterical.

And Shaw knew why.

"Drive to the precinct now," Shaw ordered the driver. "Ms. Carr can see the doctor there."

He had to get Sabrina to safety and put her in protective custody. Because those gunmen would try to eliminate any and all witnesses.

And that meant they would come after Sabrina to finish what they had started.

Chapter Four

"You can wait in my office," Shaw said to her the moment Sabrina came out of the ladies' room.

He motioned for her to follow him down the glossy tiled corridor that was lined with fallen officers' photos and department commendations.

His voice sounded so professional. So detached. And Sabrina couldn't help but notice that he didn't touch her. He hadn't since they were in the car driving away from that building where Shaw had rescued her. From the moment they'd stepped out of the vehicle and into SAPD headquarters, he'd kept at least several inches of distance between them.

"Thank you, for everything," she managed to say, though she didn't know how. Her mouth was trembling, and the words came out shaky, as well.

When Shaw finally stopped walking and

pointed to the open room, Sabrina stepped into the large office with an ornate desk nameplate that had Captain Shaw Tolbert scrolled on it. The nameplate and the office were reminders that Shaw was an important man in SAPD. A leader.

And he had better things to do than babysit her.

"While you were in the bathroom, I had some food brought in for you," Shaw explained. He tipped his head to the bottle of water and wrapped sandwich that had come from a vending machine. "Yeah, I know it's not very appetizing, but I figured you'd be hungry and dehydrated."

"The gunmen gave us water," she mumbled.

No food, though. Despite not having eaten for about ten hours, she wasn't hungry, but she sat in the leather chair next to his desk and opened the water and sandwich anyway. Both tasted like dust. But she continued to eat because the baby needed this.

"Did the gunmen hurt you, physically?" he asked.

She lifted her wrist so he could see the marks. "Just a bruise or two from where one of them grabbed me. That was the peppermint guy who did that. He chewed on breath mints during most of the standoff, and he threw some of the wrappers on the floor."

Shaw took out a notepad from his desk and jotted that down.

"Do you need to bag my clothes so you can check for fibers or anything?" she asked.

"I'll get them later. For now, just eat." Shaw took out his phone and asked whomever he called for a situation report.

While he listened to that report, Shaw stood there so stoically. He looked the ultimate professional. And for just a second, she was reminded of the first time she'd seen him at a fundraiser dinner nearly eight years ago. She and Fay had gone with dates, but the minute they'd spotted the "hot cop" as Fay had called him, they'd both flirted with him.

Shaw had flirted back.

He truly had been a hot cop. Still was, she reluctantly admitted. With his classic good looks all mixed together with a touch of bad boy, he was every woman's fantasy.

More than a little tipsy that night eight years ago, Fay and she had drawn cocktails straws for dibs on who would go after him. Fay had won. But even after all this time, Sabrina couldn't help but wonder what her life would be like if she hadn't drawn the short straw that night.

"Your doctor's on the way," Shaw let her know, ending the call.

He didn't come back into his office. He stood in the doorway but fired glances all around. Probably because the headquarters building was buzzing with activity from the hostage situation, and he was trying to keep abreast of what was going on. Or maybe because he didn't want to be too close to her. Nadine Duggan's death was likely bringing back memories. Bad memories. Of Fay.

And of Sabrina.

"Go ahead. You can leave." Sabrina tried to make it sound like an order. She took another bite of the sandwich. "I'll be fine."

That was a lie. He knew it. So did she. But Shaw still turned and walked away.

"I have to see someone for a minute," he said from over his shoulder.

Sabrina soon saw the reason for his quick exit. Along with several other officers, Lieutenant Bo Duggan was just up the hall, and Shaw went to them.

She watched them through the open doorway, but she couldn't hear their conversation. She didn't need to. Shaw laid his hand on Bo's arm and no doubt offered words of sympathy, something that Shaw knew all about. He was almost certainly remembering Fay's death.

Sabrina remembered it, too.

Bo's wife had died under perhaps violent circumstances, or at least terrifying ones while being a hostage by those gunmen. Fay had chosen her own death. Well, her depression had chosen it for her anyway. Still, the final result was the death of a loved one.

"You shouldn't have gone off your antidepressants," Sabrina mumbled to Fay, who, of course, could no longer hear her.

Sabrina had said the same words to her while Fay had been alive. Fay hadn't listened—because the antidepressants couldn't be taken with the meds necessary for Fay to harvest her eggs for the in vitro procedure for the surrogate. And that surrogate was none other than Sabrina since Fay couldn't carry a child.

A baby at any cost, Fay had said.

Sabrina had argued with her, had even considered telling her best friend that the surrogacy offer was off the table so that Fay would go back on her meds. But Fay hadn't listened to that, either. Sabrina had lost the argument.

Fay had gone through with the harvesting, only to learn that none of her eggs was viable. That's when Sabrina had volunteered to use her own eggs. Shaw had agreed, reluctantly, and only to appease Fay, but there hadn't been time to finish what they started. Because of the long-term effect of going without her meds, Fay had taken her own life before Sabrina could get pregnant.

Some women would have stopped there. Some women wouldn't have continued to press to carry a baby for a dead friend. But she owed Fay. She owed Shaw. And that's why three months after Fay's death, Sabrina had pressured Shaw for her to use the embryos that Shaw and she had created. It hadn't been an easy fight—especially since the embryos were her DNA, not Fay's. However, in the end Shaw had agreed, probably because he'd been too beaten down by Fay's death to realize the full impact of having a baby with Sabrina.

Well, he no doubt knew the full impact now.

Sabrina certainly did. Yes, she'd owed Shaw and Fay. She'd owed them this child, but there were consequences for delivering on a promise to a dying friend.

One of those consequences was headed her way. Shaw was walking back toward her. Alone. Bo was going in the other direction, no doubt so he could start handling the aftermath of his wife's death.

"How's Bo doing?" she asked the moment Shaw returned.

"How do you think he's doing?" Shaw snapped, then he cursed under his breath and mumbled something that sounded like an apology.

He still didn't come in the room with her. But she got his visual attention. Shaw bracketed his hands on both sides of the doorway and stared at her. "Your doctor's in the building, and she'll be here any minute."

"There's no hurry. I wasn't injured. I'm not having any cramps or anything."

"That's good." A moment later, he repeated it. "I just got a situation report from one of my sergeants. Still no sign of the gunmen, but we'll find them." He was back to sounding professional, as if giving her a briefing.

"Do you need to take my statement now?"

"It can wait until morning. All the interview rooms are already being used."

Yes. Because there were so many witnesses.

So many victims.

"On the drive over, one of those calls I made was to start the process to get background checks on all the hospital employees, including Michael Frost, the person who phoned you

about the emergency meeting," Shaw continued. "We've also gathered all the hostages'
cell phones we can find. They'd been tossed
behind the desk in the nurses' station."

"Yes. The gunmen took them from us within
the first few minutes of the standoff."

"I figured they had. We'll check to see if
the gunmen used any of them."

"They had their own phones," she remembered. "I don't think they used any of ours.
And they didn't use the hospital phones,
either."

He nodded. "Is it possible one of the hostages was able to use their cell to take a picture of either of the men?"

Sabrina thought about that a moment, forcing herself to mentally return to the chaos
that'd happened on that fourth floor. "It's possible, but I didn't see it happen. Besides, they
wore ski masks the entire time."

He opened his mouth, no doubt to continue
this coplike questioning, but he stopped when
his phone buzzed again. No call this time, but
a text message. When he read it, Shaw cursed
and scrubbed his hand over his face.

Despite the wobbly legs, Sabrina stood.
"What's wrong?"

Shaw put the phone away, and his grip
tightened on the doorjamb. "Another of the

hostages died—a woman who'd given birth. And one of the newborns is missing. We just issued an Amber Alert."

"Missing? How? There were only two gunmen, and when they took me from the hospital and to that other building, they didn't have a baby with them."

"Maybe they moved the child before they took you. Maybe the baby was already in the vehicle." The briefing was over, and the raw emotion was coming through his voice. "We don't have any suspects in custody, and we don't even have a motive for the crime."

Maybe it was his stark frustration or maybe it was her exhaustion, but Sabrina was sorry she'd stood. She nearly lost her balance and caught on to the desk to steady herself.

That got Shaw moving. He hurried to her, took her by the arm and put her back in the chair. But he did more than that. He put his hand on her arm, much as he'd done to Bo. And then he looked down at her. However, he didn't get much further than that look.

There was a knock at the door, and Shaw spun around, obviously grateful for the interruption. Sabrina suddenly felt grateful as well because it was her OB, Dr. Claire Nicholson.

"Sabrina," the doctor greeted. "I came as quickly as I could."

"I need to make some calls," Shaw volunteered, and he headed out after giving the doctor a brief nod.

Dr. Nicholson watched Shaw leave and then eased the door shut. While she opened her medical bag, she studied Sabrina's face.

"He's the baby's father," the doctor commented. Dr. Nicholson knew that, of course, because she had also been the one to implant the embryos in Sabrina. "He's worried about you."

Sabrina nearly laughed. "He's worried about the baby, that's all."

"At this point, it's nearly impossible to separate mom from the baby. He's worried about *you*," the doctor confirmed and took out the fetoscope, something Sabrina was familiar with. It was a modified stethoscope used to listen to the baby's heartbeat. The doctor positioned it on her own forehead and motioned for Sabrina to lift her top.

"Any contractions or spotting?" the doctor asked.

"No. Just some Braxton Hicks." Thank God. Other than the practice contractions and being jittery and exhausted, she truly was okay. Now, mentally, well, that was a different story.

Sabrina winced a little when the cool plastic-coated metal touched her belly. The doctor moved it around, paused several moments and then smiled.

"That's a good strong heartbeat." She pulled off the fetoscope and put it back into the bag. "Of course, I'd like to do an ultrasound, but that can wait a day or two." She took out a manual blood pressure kit and used it on Sabrina's arm. "It's slightly high but considering the circumstances, I'm not surprised. Do you have someone to stay with tonight?"

No. She didn't. But Sabrina nodded anyway. "I'll be fine." It was her standard response, one she'd been saying her entire life, she realized.

Tonight it wasn't true. She wouldn't be fine because those gunmen were still out there.

There was a quick knock at the door, and it opened, slowly. Shaw peeked inside. "Everything okay?" Shaw's attention went right to her and stayed there.

The doctor looked at Sabrina before she answered. "Sabrina and the baby are both *fine*. In about four weeks, you'll both have a healthy newborn. But for now, Sabrina needs rest. You can make sure that happens?"

Sabrina got to her feet, to protest Dr. Nicholson dumping this on Shaw, but that's when she noticed why Shaw was staring at her. Her top was still bunched up, and her pregnant belly was bare. She quickly righted her top.

"Rest," the doctor ordered Sabrina, and she stepped around Shaw so she could leave.

"You don't need to keep checking on me," Sabrina insisted.

"I've already arranged a hotel room for you," Shaw let her know. He glanced again at her now-covered belly and swallowed hard. "Does it hurt?"

Sabrina shook her head. "Does what hurt?"

"The baby, when it kicks."

"Oh. No. Not really." She shrugged, puzzled by the abrupt change of subject. "Well, unless she connects with my kidney or something."

Shaw's left eyebrow shot up. *"She?"*

Sabrina shook her head even harder. "I don't know the baby's sex. I wanted to keep it a surprise. *She* just sounds better than *it*."

"Right." He stepped to the side. "Come on. I'll get you to the hotel."

Since this was already more than awkward, Sabrina didn't argue, but as soon as Shaw had her stashed away at the hotel, she would insist that he leave. If he felt forced to spend time with her, it would only make him hate her more.

"Thank you," she told him. She walked out of the office ahead of him, but there was someone waiting outside the door. It was a lanky built cop wearing a crisp blue uniform.

Shaw groaned softly, probably because there was a look of concern on the man's face. "More bad news, Officer Newell?"

He handed Shaw several sheets of paper that had been stapled together. "That's the preliminary background checks you asked for on the hospital employees. Oh, and a guy keeps calling here, asking to speak to Ms. Carr. He said his name is Gavin Cunningham."

Shaw looked up from the papers he'd just received and turned to Sabrina, obviously wanting an explanation. Was it her imagination or did he seem a little jealous that another man would be phoning her? But she rethought that.

Shaw could never be jealous of her.

"Gavin Cunningham's a client," she explained to the other officer. "And yes, he's persistent. I'm head of an organization called Rootsfind that helps adopted and foster kids locate their biological families, and he wants me to help him find his father. Please tell him I'll call him in a day or two."

"I already told him you weren't available, but he said it was a matter of life or death."

Sabrina and Shaw had already started to walk away, but that stopped them. Shaw stared at her, apparently waiting for an answer.

But Sabrina didn't have one. "Gavin called yesterday and sounded frantic and stressed. He said that he needed me to find his father immediately. He wanted to meet with me right then, but I had other appointments. I told him I'd see him today. That obviously didn't happen because I was taken hostage."

"Well, he asked me to give you his number, just in case you'd forgotten it." The officer reached in his pocket and extracted a notepad-sized piece of paper with the number on it.

"Thanks. I'll call him on the way to the hotel."

"You think it's that critical to call him back tonight? Because it can wait," Shaw added, not giving her a chance to answer. He nudged her to get her moving and continued to read the papers the officer had given him. "Unless you think it's possible this client is suicidal?"

Sabrina gave that some thought. "I didn't see any warning signs that he's contemplating suicide."

"Right," he mumbled.

She didn't miss the accusing tone. Shaw

seemed to be saying—*as if you'd recognize those warning signs.* She certainly hadn't with Fay. "He's just a little more obsessed than most about finding his father."

Sabrina knew something about that, as well. Since she'd been adopted at birth, she'd spent most of her life looking for her biological parents. She'd failed. And it was the reason she had created Rootsfind. Sometimes, the desire to find those DNA roots just burned hotter in some people.

Shaw folded the papers that Officer Newell had given him, and he led her out of the building and into the open parking garage where there were dozens of police vehicles. "I know you're tired, but I need you to think back to the person who called you about that moms' support group meeting?"

"Michael Frost," she supplied.

"You're sure that's who called you?"

"Positive. Why?"

"Because according to hospital records, they don't have an employee by that name."

Oh, mercy. Had this man been in on it? Had he lured her to the hospital? "I thought something was strange about that call. I mean, he made the meeting sound like an emergency, as if Nadine were in some kind of trouble."

"You didn't phone Nadine first to try to verify what was wrong?"

"No." And she suddenly felt stupid for not doing just that. "Shaw, I'm sorry. Because I didn't follow my instincts about that call, I put the baby in danger."

Other than a sound in his throat that could have meant anything, or nothing, he didn't react. "This Michael Frost called you on your cell phone?"

"No. The office line."

"Then I'll have it checked for all incoming calls. We might get lucky." He got her inside one of the vehicles and drove away. "Stay low in the seat," he instructed.

That got her heart pounding again. "What if the gunmen are lurking around out here, watching us? What if they try to follow us?"

"I'll make sure that doesn't happen. That's why I'll have to drive around for a while even though the hotel is just up the street."

She had no idea how long *a while* would be, but maybe she could get some things done. Important things. She'd ignored her instincts about the call from Michael Frost, but she wouldn't do that with Cunningham.

"Could I use your phone to call Gavin?"

she asked Shaw. "Just in case he does have suicide on his mind."

Shaw took out his phone and passed it to her, her fingers grazing his. For some reason, that tiny touch packed a wallop, and it took Sabrina a moment to gather her breath.

"Or maybe I shouldn't use your cell because your name will show up on Cunningham's caller ID," she reconsidered.

"That phone is clean, only the number will show up, and he won't be able to trace it back to me or SAPD," Shaw explained. He took a turn and kept his attention fastened to the rearview mirror.

Sabrina nodded again and pressed in the numbers. Gavin Cunningham answered on the first ring. "This is Sabrina Carr," she greeted. She, too, checked the mirrors to make sure no one was following them.

"Thank God you're all right," Gavin said immediately. "When I saw the hostages on the news, I thought of you. And I tried to call you, but there was no answer at your office or your home. You must have been scared to death."

She debated how much she should say and settled for, "I was rescued."

"Good. That's good." He paused. "Can we meet?"

She didn't have to debate that. "No. I'm still tied up with police business. I called because you told Officer Newell it was a matter of life and death, that you had to speak to me. Gavin, what's going on?"

He paused so long, but she could hear his breathing. It was fast and uneven. Maybe Shaw had been right about Gavin being suicidal, and just in case he was, she pressed the speaker function so that Shaw would be able to hear the rest of the conversation. "I can't talk about this over the phone," he finally answered. "I just need to see you."

Sabrina ignored that request. "Where are you right now?"

"At my house," he whispered. "You can't come?"

"No."

"All right, then. Sorry I bothered you. I'm sorry about everything."

And he hung up.

Shaw cursed, took the phone and punched in some numbers. "Officer Newell," Shaw said to the person he'd called. "I need someone to do a welfare check on that Gavin Cunningham, the man who kept calling Ms. Carr. He's at his residence, and I want someone over there immediately. Let me know what you find out."

Shaw brought the car to a stop beneath the canopied entrance of the Riverfront Hotel. There was a man dressed in a suit in front, apparently waiting for them, and he got into the car and drove away after Shaw and she exited. Shaw ushered her inside the lobby where another person, probably a plainclothes officer, handed Shaw a room key.

"I'm still not safe, am I?" she asked as they got on the elevator.

"You are now." Shaw didn't say another word until the elevator stopped. He didn't waste any time. He hurried her to the room and got her inside.

"Get some sleep," he said, pointing to the only bed in the small room. He closed the door.

Sabrina glanced at the bed, at the small no-frills standard hotel room, and then at him. "Will the officer in the lobby be able to stand guard outside my door?" Suddenly, the thought of being alone—and unprotected— was terrifying. She slid her hand over her belly.

"No." And Shaw didn't add anything to that for several long moments. Then he reached back and set both locks on the door. "The officer is arranging to have some clothes and toiletries sent up, and then he'll report back to headquarters. We're short staffed on the investigation. There are a lot of witnesses to interview. A lot of women who'll need protection."

"Including me," she mumbled.

He nodded. "I'll be staying with you. Until we catch the gunmen, you'll be in my protective custody."

Sabrina's mouth dropped open. "You're going to stay here, with me, *alone?*"

The muscles stirred in his jaw. "Yeah. Now get some rest."

Fat chance of that. "But you must have a ton of work to do. Surely someone else can do this."

Even though she wanted Shaw to be the one. Well, sort of. She knew he'd do anything to protect the baby, and that was a huge plus, but being in such close quarters with Shaw would only make her remember that he was indeed a *hot cop.*

Sabrina cursed herself. Damn hormones. Through much of this pregnancy, she'd been thinking about Shaw, and she hadn't thought of him as her baby's father, either. But as a lover.

As if that would ever happen.

Still, her hormones had persisted.

Like now, for instance.

Yes, she was so tired she could hardly stand, but she felt the trickle of heat go through her, and she wished they were friendly or intimate enough for him to hold her.

"What's wrong?" he asked. "You're breathing hard."

"Am I?" Sabrina tried to fix that, but she didn't think she was successful. "I have to go to the bathroom."

And she got away from him as fast as she could. She used the facilities and went to the sink to wash her hands and toss some cold water on her face.

"He's Fay's husband," she reminded herself. But her body only reminded her that Fay was dead, and her friend would have been the last person to want Shaw and her to stay apart.

Take care of Shaw for me.

That was the message Fay had left on Sabrina's answering machine. The moment Sabrina had come in from work and heard the weakened voice and the slurred words, she'd known something was horribly wrong. She'd tried to call Fay, of course, but it was already too late. Shaw had answered the phone to say that Fay had just died in his arms.

She blinked back the tears, and the old memories. Shaw had been so angry. So hurt.

Heck, he was still angry and hurt after all these months.

The baby kicked, a flurry of flutters, and she smiled in spite of the mess she'd made of her life. Then, she braced herself and went back into the room.

Shaw glanced at her, but he didn't have time to say anything because his phone buzzed. "Captain Tolbert," he answered.

Since this would likely be the first of many calls about the investigation, Sabrina went ahead and kicked off her shoes and pulled back the cover. She was so tired she could fall asleep despite the circumstances.

Shaw's expression had her rethinking that.

"Repeat that," Shaw insisted. Several moments went by before he barked, "Find him."

"What's wrong?" Sabrina asked, but she was afraid to hear the answer. There'd already been so much bad news.

Shaw shoved his phone back into his pocket. "A unit arrived at Gavin Cunningham's place a few minutes ago. The door was wide open, so the officer went inside."

Sabrina held her breath. "Is Gavin dead?"

"No. He wasn't there. Neither was his car, and the neighbor said he sped away about a half hour ago. He was going so fast that he knocked down the neighbor's mailbox, and he didn't even stop."

Even though that didn't sound good, many things could have caused him to do that. A family emergency. Or a sudden illness. But judging from Shaw's expression, it was neither of those things.

"He left a note," Shaw added, "for you." He walked closer and eased down on the bed beside her. He met her eye to eye. "Sabrina, just how well do you know this man?"

She shook her head and held her breath. "Not well at all, only what I've already told you. Why? What did the note say?"

"Gavin Cunningham said he was sorry, that it was his fault you were taken hostage."

Chapter Five

The sound woke Shaw.

His eyes flew open, and he sat up from his slumping position in the chair. In the same motion he reached for his gun, which he'd placed on the nightstand. His training and experience caused him to expect the worst.

An intruder.

Or the gunmen who'd escaped.

The lamp was still on in the far corner of the room, so he had no trouble seeing that there were no intruders or gunmen. Sabrina and he were very much alone, but she was no longer sound asleep as she had been that last time he'd checked on her. She was fighting with the comforter and sheets.

"Owwww!" She got out from beneath the covers and tried to stand.

"What's wrong?" Shaw jumped up from the chair. "Are you in labor?"

She shook her head, but her face was twisted with pain. "Foot cramp."

He glanced down and saw that the toes on her left foot were rigid. "Put some pressure on it," he suggested, and he looped his arm around her waist so he could help her keep her balance.

Shaw forced himself to calm down, but it wasn't easy. He'd braced himself for a fight, and even though he was glad there wasn't one, it would still take him a while to absorb the jolt of adrenaline.

Sabrina adjusted her weight, so she could press her foot to the floor, and all the while she continued to say "owww."

"Pregnancy," she grumbled. "I get these stupid things every night."

Every night? Sheez. Shaw actually felt sorry for her.

And guilty.

He had no idea she'd been going through this. He'd read about possible pregnancy symptoms, of course, but he just hadn't made the personal connection between Sabrina and those symptoms. With her squirming and groaning in pain, it was an eye opener.

So was Sabrina, for that matter.

The clothes she'd worn while a hostage were now bagged and in the corner ready for pickup. She was dressed in a white cotton gown that the department had scrounged up for her.

Thin, white cotton.

Not at all meant to be provocative, but on her pregnant body, it hugged every inch of her, including her fuller breasts and bottom. Yes, she was pregnant, but that didn't stop him from responding to her.

And that made him feel even guiltier.

Sabrina was hands-off in every sense of the word.

"Thanks," she mumbled, her face relaxing a little.

They were hip to hip, with his arm slung around her, and she glanced down at the physical contact between them.

"Sorry." Shaw moved away. "I didn't want you to fall."

"I wasn't complaining. Actually, I was savoring the moment." But then her eyes widened. "I didn't mean it like that. Uh, I'm not really sure what I meant. It's just been a while since I've had a man's arm around me, that's all."

Since Shaw didn't know what to say to that, he settled for, "Yeah."

Her cheeks flushed, and she splayed her hands on her belly. "You're probably thinking it would be impossible for a man to get his arms around me, right?" She chuckled, but the humor was just an attempt to diffuse the situation.

Shaw needed it diffused. He could see the outline of her nipples, and he felt that tug below the belt. It was a basic male reaction, he assured himself, and he told that tug to get lost.

Sabrina sat back down on the bed and shook her head. "Yeah, I know. I look disgusting."

"No. You don't." Shaw decided to leave it at that.

She seemed relieved, or something. Her face relaxed anyway. "I have stretch marks. Three of them. Four," she added after a shrug. "Sometimes, I don't think my body will ever go back to normal."

"It will." Shaw wanted to hit himself. He didn't know much about this pregnancy stuff and should just shut up.

So that he'd do just that, he looked back at the laptop he had sitting next to his chair. It'd been delivered along with Sabrina's gown and toiletries, and Shaw had been using it to get updates throughout the night. It was nearly 6:00 a.m. so a new update should be arriving shortly.

"Don't get me wrong. I'm so happy to be

pregnant," she continued. "I mean, this baby is a miracle as far as I'm concerned. And trust me, I'm a big believer in miracles."

She groaned again, and that drew Shaw's attention right back to her. Sabrina was looking down at her belly.

"My miracle is awake," she mumbled. "And playing soccer with my kidneys."

Shaw looked at her belly, too, and saw the movement. He shifted to the edge of his chair for a better look. "I can actually see the kicks."

"Oh, yes. You can see them." She laughed. It was rich and thick as if she was sharing his amazement, though she no doubt experienced this many times a day.

Sabrina reached out, latched on to his hand and pressed it against her stomach.

Shaw almost pulled back. It was an automatic response when it came to Sabrina. But the baby moves stopped him. That was his baby inside her. A miracle, indeed. And he or she was kicking like crazy.

Amazed, Shaw looked up at Sabrina. Their gazes connected. She was smiling, and Shaw realized he was, too.

Her smile hit him harder than a heavy weight could have.

He drew back his hand. He drew himself

back as well and moved deeper into the chair so there'd be some distance between them. This was such an incredible moment, and it was a moment he should have been sharing with his late wife.

Not Sabrina.

"Right," Sabrina mumbled. Her smile vanished, and she didn't roll her eyes, but it was close. "This is about Fay."

"Don't," he warned, certain there wasn't a trace of his smile left, either.

"Don't," she repeated. She got up, started for the bathroom, but then stopped. She kept her back to him. "I miss Fay, too. I miss her every minute of every day. And every one of those minutes I hate myself for not cramming those antidepressants in her mouth. Or for not being there when she overdosed and took her life. I don't need you to punish me, Shaw, because I swear to you, I've done a pretty good job of punishing myself."

She didn't give him a chance to respond. She went into the bathroom and shut the door.

Hell.

Shaw felt lower than dirt. Yes, he was still angry with Sabrina. Always would be. And he would always put some of the blame for Fay's death on her shoulders. But after what Sabrina had been through in the past fifteen hours, she didn't need him adding to her stress.

He went to the bathroom door and knocked. "I'm sorry."

The words seemed foreign to him, and he realized why. It was the first time he'd ever said those two words to Sabrina. It had been so easy to hang on to his anger and hurt when she'd been out of sight, but with her right on the other side of that door, and probably crying, Shaw knew he was soon going to have to come to terms with her and the baby.

But how?

How did he come to terms with having Sabrina in his life when having her there felt as if he were betraying Fay?

He heard the water running in the sink, and several moments later, the door opened. She ducked around him, dodging his gaze, but he saw the red eyes.

Yep, he'd made her cry.

Maybe he should just hit himself in the head with a rock. It might make him feel better.

"What's the latest on the case?" she asked.

Shaw didn't really want to have the conversation he was about to launch into, but it was time to clear the air. Well, partly. He just needed to get Sabrina and him to a place where…where…

But he couldn't finish that.

He just didn't want all this emotion eating up the air between them.

Shaw caught her arm and turned her around to face him. "This baby is a miracle for me, too," he told her. "I want to be a father. Always have. And it doesn't matter that we're not… friends…or whatever, we'll make this work." He frowned, not liking the sound of that.

And why the hell was he hemming and hawing?

He wasn't the hemming and hawing type.

"We'll make the *shared custody* work," he amended.

She nodded, and her chin came up. He recognized that gesture and knew it was all for show. He also saw the tears that still watered her eyes.

"Pregnancy hormones," she complained and swiped away the tears.

Shaw mumbled another, "Hell." And before he could talk himself out of it, he pulled her into his arms much as he'd done in the car after he'd rescued her from that abandoned building.

But this was way different.

In the car, they'd been side by side. Now,

they were face-to-face. The baby was between them, of course, but it was still body to body contact. That contact got even closer when her head dropped to his shoulder. She whispered something he couldn't understand, didn't *want* to understand, and her hot breath hit against his neck.

That tug below his belt became a strong pull.

Oh, man.

It'd been months since he'd had a woman, and his body was reminding him of that.

Sabrina slid her arms around him, drawing him closer. He gritted his teeth but didn't back away. He owed her a little TLC. But it wasn't TLC that kept going through his mind.

Was traditional sex even possible when a woman was eight months pregnant? Heck. He didn't care if it was traditional. His body was starting to suggest other possibilities.

"Yes," he heard Sabrina say, and for one heart-stopping moment, he thought he'd asked that traditional sex question aloud.

Shaw pulled back and looked at her.

She looked up at him. Frowned. Then, cursed. "Yes, I'm aroused," she whispered as if confessing to a murder. She glanced down at her nipples, and with the thin, snug cotton, he could see those nipples were puckered. "Sorry about that."

Again, he was speechless. But not numb. Hell, he was aroused, too.

"It's the pregnancy hormones again. Foot cramps, crying spells and the libido of a teenage boy. A libido I haven't acted on, by the way." She turned away from him again and groaned. "And I'm so sorry for telling you that. Don't worry. I'm not asking you to do anything about it."

Too bad. His body was ready to help her out, even though his mind was pulling him back. But Shaw knew from experience that a man's mind rarely won out in situations like this. If this had been any woman other than Sabrina, he would have tested the logistics of having sex during the last trimester of pregnancy.

"What's happening with the case?" she repeated.

He just stared at her. Or rather he stared at her backside. And the air continued to stir, hot and thick, around them. And hot and thick was exactly how he felt.

"Any news about my client, Gavin Cunningham?" Sabrina pressed, obviously determined to have a *normal* conversation. She took her replacement shirt from off the end of the bed and put it on over her gown.

Shaw shook off the effects of his own suddenly raging libido so he could get his mind on anything but the thought of what it would feel like to be deep inside Sabrina.

"We still haven't been able to find Gavin," Shaw finally managed to say. "Have you come up with any possible reason why he would think it was his fault that you were taken hostage?"

She downed some water from the bottle on the nightstand. "This is a stretch, but maybe he knew the gunmen. He said nothing to me to indicate that, but I can't come up with a connection between a Rootsfind client and what went on at the hospital."

Shaw thought about that a moment. "What exactly did Gavin want you to do for him?"

She shrugged as if the answer were obvious. The shrug caused her shirt to shift, and he got another peek at her nipples.

Shaw looked away.

"He wanted me to find his birth father," Sabrina explained, "and he gave me all the normal details—his place and date of birth. His mother's name. She was a single mom and died young without revealing who his father was."

"You said Gavin was persistent, more obsessed than most about finding his parent. Why? Had something changed recently in his life? Like maybe he needed bone marrow or something?"

She shook her head. "He didn't mention that, but I suppose it's possible. Still…" She paused. "I got the feeling this was more personal than medical. He seemed angry that his father hadn't made himself known."

Interesting. It might not be connected to the case, but Shaw would dig deeper. He wanted to learn why Gavin felt responsible for Sabrina being taken hostage. That might be the key to solving all of this.

"I've been getting updates throughout the night," Shaw explained. "That nurse, Michael Frost, called at least two of the other hostages, Willa Marks and Bailey Hodges. Neither was part of the moms' support group, but he told them their doctors had gotten back critical lab results and that they needed to come to the hospital immediately."

Sabrina made a sharp intake of breath. "So, it was a trick. And I fell for it."

Shaw didn't want her to go back to beating herself up. Hell, he probably would have fallen for it, too. "Is it possible that Michael Frost was one of the gunmen?"

She stayed quiet a moment. "The breath mint guy did most of the talking, and he didn't sound like Frost. Of course, he could have disguised his voice."

Absolutely. Shaw was looking into that, too, but it might be a dead end since none of the messages had been recorded.

Shaw sat in the chair across from her so they could be eye to eye. And wouldn't be touching. "Do you know if you had anything in common with Willa Marks or Bailey Hodges, the other two women that Frost called? Maybe you met them before the hostage situation."

Again, she paused, and her forehead bunched up while she stayed deep in thought. "I don't think so. I heard the gunmen calling out for someone named Bailey, of course, but this is the first I've heard of Willa Marks. I'm pretty sure I've never met either of them."

There might still be a connection that could come out later. For now, he needed as many solid leads and facts as possible.

He took some paper from the briefcase that'd been delivered with the laptop, and handed it and a pen to Sabrina. "Why don't you start writing down your statement? I'll arrange to have us some breakfast delivered."

The sun had barely come up, but his body was already screaming for caffeine. And sex.

It wasn't going to get the sex, but he could do something about the coffee.

He used his cell to call headquarters and request breakfast. The hotel had room service, but it was too big of a risk to use it. Sabrina's face had been plastered all over the news by now, and he didn't want a hotel employee recognizing her and blabbing to his friends. News like that could get back to the gunmen.

Sabrina was already busy writing her statement when he finished the call so Shaw settled back into the chair to check the messages on his secure laptop. He'd barely made it through the first one when his phone buzzed.

"It's Officer Newell," the caller identified himself. "We caught a break on the surveillance cameras we took from the hospital. Most had been disabled. Nothing sophisticated. The gunmen had smashed them, but they missed a newly installed one at the end of the hall near the lab."

Shaw wanted to cheer. Finally, some good news. "What do we have?"

"Neither of the men took off their ski masks so we don't have images to put through the facial recognition software, but we do have some of their movements. One of them went into the lab, just as several of the witnesses said. And he took one of the hostages with him. A computer tech named Willa Marks. He appears to have forced her to help him look for something. They were going through the files."

"Any fingerprints on the keyboards?"

"Plenty. But both of the gunmen wore surgical gloves. And even though there's a lot of trace on the computer and the surrounding area, it'll take us a while to rule out what belongs to the staff or the hostage Willa Marks, and what might belong to the gunmen."

Newell was right. That type of sorting might take days or even weeks, especially when dozens of people would have to be excluded. "What's Ms. Marks saying? Does she know why the gunman had her in there with him?"

"She's, uh, not able to talk. She received a head injury when the gunman shoved her down as she was trying to escape. She doesn't remember anything."

Hell. The more he heard, the more his stomach clenched. And this was just the beginning. How many more sickening details were there?

Since Willa Marks might not be able to tell them what had happened, at least for a while, Shaw needed to piece together as much as he could. "What files did the gunman search?"

Sabrina stopped writing and stared at him, obviously waiting for an update.

"We're trying to sort that out now," Officer Newell verified. "They accessed at least four dozen files, but we don't know why. I can tell you that all the files they accessed dealt with DNA."

"DNA?" Shaw questioned. "What kind of DNA?"

"Some were from the babies, some from the parents. We're talking court-ordered DNA tests. Others were apparently done for medical reasons, like for a baby needing a transplant. A few more are for a database for umbilical storage. There were even a few samples that SAPD had outsourced to the lab for processing."

Shaw went still. "Were any for paternity?" he questioned.

"Yes, sir. There were several of those. One of them court ordered, as well. Why, what are you thinking?"

He was thinking the gunmen might have wanted to confirm that Sabrina's baby was his. So the baby could be used as *leverage*.

But leverage for what?

Because if he could figure that out, he could figure out who was behind all of this.

"Let me call you back," Shaw told the

officer. "I need to ask Sabrina a few questions. In the meantime, find out if the gunmen tampered with any of those files or if they got access to the DNA samples themselves. Specifically, look for any files that were removed or deleted. The tech should be able to do that in just a couple of minutes."

"I'll tell him," Newell assured him.

"What about paternity?" Sabrina asked the moment Shaw ended the call.

She already looked worried, and he didn't want to make that worry worse, but he couldn't shield her from this. Sabrina might very well have information they could put together with what the police knew, and then they might have the big picture.

That big picture could lead them to make an arrest.

"The gunmen were going through the DNA files," Shaw told her. "Is it possible our baby's DNA was there?"

"Maybe." She swallowed hard. "I had to have an amniocentesis done. That's a test where they draw some fluid from around the baby and test it for abnormalities."

"Why did you have that done?" He felt stupid for not knowing.

"Because I got really sick with pneumonia during my second month of pregnancy. I didn't tell you because I didn't want you to worry. You already had a lot on your mind what with adjusting to being a father, and I didn't want to add to it. Anyway, my OB wanted to make sure the baby hadn't been harmed from all the meds. She wasn't," she quickly added. "The doctor said everything was fine. But the amniotic fluid would contain DNA, and it's probably on file at the hospital."

And if the gunmen had that file, that was likely the reason they had taken Sabrina with them when they fled the hospital. They'd wanted Sabrina and the proof that the baby she was carrying was his.

Well, they didn't have Sabrina. He did. But that didn't mean they wouldn't try to get her again so they could force him to do something.

His phone buzzed again, and when he saw Newell's name on the screen, Shaw answered it as quickly as he could.

"You were right," Newell said, "the tech didn't have any trouble finding the files that'd been deleted. There were three of them. One wasn't labeled, but you'll recognize both names of the two we could identify. One was for Sabrina Carr."

Shaw silently cursed. "And the other?"

"Her client, Gavin Cunningham."

"Cunningham?" Shaw repeated. He didn't like the way the man's name kept popping up in this investigation. "Why was his DNA at the hospital?"

"We're not sure. There was no code to indicate why the file was even there. It wasn't even logged in properly through official channels. But it was his name on the file itself."

Another dead end, except this dead end could be reopened once they had Cunningham. "Put every agency in the state on alert. I want Cunningham found *immediately*."

He glanced at Sabrina who was looking very concerned again. Shaw knew how she felt. He had to question Cunningham.

"Breakfast will be here soon," he said, checking his watch. "I need to wash up before it arrives. Why don't you go ahead and work on your statement? We can go through it after we eat."

She nodded but didn't look at all convinced that she'd be able to concentrate. Again, Shaw knew exactly how she felt, but he had to clear his head before more evidence started pouring in.

He went into the bathroom, but he'd no sooner stepped inside when he heard the noise.

It was a crashing sound.

The sounds of wood and metal being bashed.

Shaw turned, ready to react, but the bathroom door slammed shut when the hotel room door smacked into it.

Someone had broken in.

He shoved at the door, but it was blocked. Shaw rammed his shoulder against it, hard. It still didn't budge.

"Sabrina?" he called out while he tried again.

She didn't answer, but the sound she made tore right through him.

Sabrina screamed.

Chapter Six

Sabrina didn't have any warning of the danger. Just seconds earlier, Shaw had gone into the bathroom to the right of the room entrance. Mere seconds. And then the hotel room door flew open.

The man who came rushing through was wearing a ski mask.

He was also armed.

Worse, he was literally using the hotel door and his body to block Shaw from coming out of the bathroom. She could hear Shaw cursing, calling out her name, and he was bashing against the door, but the gunman wasn't budging.

Sabrina automatically turned, ready to run, but there was no place for her to escape. Behind her were two windows, but they were on the third floor. Even if she could get the windows open before the gunman grabbed her, she couldn't risk jumping and hurting the baby. So, she did the only thing she could think to do.

She screamed again.

The man lifted his gun, something small and sleek and rigged with a silencer. "Come with me," he ordered. "Or I'll shoot."

The terror inside her went up a significant notch. Sabrina recognized that voice. It was the same peppermint-popping man who'd taken her hostage at the hospital. And he'd obviously come back for her.

The fear had her on the verge of panic, but Sabrina forced herself to think. Shaw's Glock was on the nightstand, and she glanced at it.

"I wouldn't do that if I were you," the man snarled. He calmly aimed his gun. Not at her.

But at the bathroom door that Shaw was battering himself against.

And he fired.

It wasn't a deafening blast, the silencer had muffled the sound to a swish, but it was a deadly sound for Sabrina.

Because the bullet could have hit Shaw.

Her heart was pounding now, and it was so loud in her ears that she couldn't tell what was going on behind that bathroom door. Shaw was still struggling, that much she could tell, but she had no idea if he was injured.

The gunman took aim at the door again. "Come here now, or I keep firing until he dies."

"Don't shoot," Sabrina practically shouted. Maybe if she was loud enough, someone would come to help. Her scream had certainly alerted the other guests. Maybe they'd already called nine-one-one. "I'll come with you."

"To hell you will," she heard Shaw yell.

Shaw rammed against the door again. The gunman aimed his weapon, no doubt with plans to shoot a second bullet at Shaw, but this time he didn't get the chance.

With a sound that was more animal than human tearing from his throat, Shaw kicked the door with a fierce jolt. The gunman flew backward and slammed into the wall.

Shaw came out after him.

The gunman had managed to keep hold of his weapon, and he tried to aim, but Shaw's fist connected with his jaw. The blow didn't disarm him, but it prevented him from firing another shot.

Shaw got off another punch, but the gunman fought back. He certainly wasn't trying to run. He bashed his gun against the side of Shaw's head.

Sabrina grabbed Shaw's Glock from the nightstand and pointed it. Not that she could fire. She didn't want to risk hitting Shaw instead.

"Captain Tolbert?" someone called out.

A moment later, the cop she'd seen at headquarters appeared in the doorway. It was Officer Newell. And he had his weapon drawn.

"Get down, Sabrina!" Shaw yelled.

Somehow, she managed to drop to her knees, and then she ducked behind the bed.

The shot blasted through the room.

"Oh, God," she prayed.

But before the last syllable had left her mouth, she heard the heavy thud of someone falling hard onto the floor.

Because it could endanger the baby, she didn't dare lift her head and see what had happened, though that's what she wanted to do. She needed to make sure Shaw hadn't been hurt.

"Are you okay?" she asked with her voice trembling.

No one answered for several long moments.

"Yeah," Shaw finally said.

That got her to her feet, and she saw the officer with his gun still aimed. He had it pointing at the masked gunman who was now sprawled out in front of the bathroom door.

Shaw leaned down and put his fingers

against the man's neck and then shook his head. The officer mumbled something under his breath and slowly lowered his gun.

"He's dead?" Sabrina asked.

Shaw nodded.

The relief was instant. Yes, there was a dead man only a few yards away from her, but the alternative could have been much worse.

But then Sabrina saw the blood trickling down the side of Shaw's head.

She hurried to him, even though he motioned for her to stay back.

"You're hurt," she let him know, and she pointed to the wound just above his left eye. No doubt where the gunman had pistol-whipped him.

"It's just a scratch." Shaw reached out, took his Glock from her and then moved her away from the body.

Behind them, Officer Newell pulled out his phone and called for assistance. And she could hear others, guests probably and maybe hotel employees, who were scurrying around in the hall. No doubt trying to get out of there and away in case there were more gunshots.

Shaw slid his arm around her waist and moved her even farther away until they were against the wall near the windows. But not directly in front of them. He closed the tiny gap in the curtains and then angled Sabrina so she wouldn't be facing the dead man.

"It's not a scratch," she said, touching her fingertips to the bruise and cut on his forehead. God knew how many other bruises he had after the multiple attempts to bash his way through the door.

"I'm fine. But I'm worried about you. About the baby," he quickly added. "Did he touch you?"

Sabrina shook her head. "It's the gunman from the hospital," she managed to say.

"You're sure?"

"Positive. I recognized his voice. He's the one who killed the hospital employee right in front of me." Her breath caught just remembering what he'd put the other women and her through. "How did he find us?"

Shaw's jaw tightened, and maybe because she was starting to shake, he eased her closer to him. Not quite a hug but close. "I don't know. But I'll figure it out." Shaw looked at Newell, who was still just outside the door and obviously standing guard. "Check and see if he has any ID on him."

Sabrina wanted to know the name of her attacker, and she only hoped the name would lead them to a motive.

"He could have just shot me," she said more

to herself than Shaw. "I wasn't armed when he broke through the door."

"He didn't want you dead. Or me."

"But he shot at you," she pointed out.

"If he'd wanted me dead, he would have aimed higher. That bullet went into the floor. Yes, it still could have been deadly, but I don't think he had killing on his mind. It's my guess he intended to kidnap you again, and then use you and the baby to get me to cooperate with something."

Yes, because that's exactly what they'd wanted when they were holding her before at the abandoned building. Some kind of leverage over Shaw. But that led her to her next question.

"Where's his partner?" she asked. Sabrina suddenly felt on the verge of panicking. "He could be in the hall, ready to strike."

Shaw used his left hand to gently take hold of her arm, and he forced her to look him in the eye. "If his partner had been here, he would have taken out Officer Newell. And he would have come in to assist with the kidnapping."

"According to his driver's license, his name is Burney Monroe," Officer Newell informed them.

"You recognize the name?" Shaw asked her.

"No."

"How about his face?" Newell continued.

She glanced past Shaw and saw that Newell had peeled back the ski mask. There was no blood on the dead man's face so she could clearly see the features. The thin nose, the square jaw, the light brown hair. In death, he certainly didn't seem menacing. He looked average.

Again she shook her head. "I don't know him."

"Probably a hired gun," Shaw provided.

That was even more chilling because the person who hired him was still out there. Or maybe his partner was the boss. She hadn't had much contact with him during the hostage situation or the kidnapping. She wasn't even sure she would recognize his voice as she had Burney Monroe's.

There was a flurry of footsteps in the hall, and Sabrina saw the second uniformed officer. "The medical examiner is on the way. CSI, too," he told Newell, and then looked at Shaw. "Sir, a squad car should be here any minute to take you and Ms. Carr to headquarters."

Good. Because it was the only place where she'd finally feel semi-safe. Of course, they had to get there first, and she certainly wouldn't breathe easy while they were out in the open.

Shaw thanked the officer, but he aimed his question at Newell. "Who made the arrangements for this hotel?"

Newell stood and shrugged. "I'm not sure, sir, but it was probably someone in Special Investigations. They're handling the security detail for the hostages."

"Find out who put us in this hotel," Shaw ordered. "I want to know the names of any officers who would have had access or direct knowledge of that information."

Newell stayed quiet a moment. "You think we have a leak or a mole in the department?" But his tone wasn't that of a question. Newell didn't believe that a breach in security was possible.

"Burney Monroe knew we were here somehow," Shaw countered. It was obvious from his expression that he didn't want to believe it, either.

Newell stooped again and patted his hands over the dead man's black windbreaker. He was looking for something, maybe a proverbial smoking gun such as written instructions from the person who had hired him and sent him here.

The person who might also be a cop.

Suddenly, being at SAPD headquarters didn't seem as appealing as it had just minutes earlier. The baby must have sensed her apprehension because she started to kick like crazy, and the muscles in Sabrina's stomach contracted. It was slightly painful, nothing she hadn't felt before, but it wasn't a good time for a bout of Braxton Hicks contractions.

Another round of contractions hit her, and Sabrina stopped so she could place her hand over her belly. She gave her baby some hopefully reassuring rubs.

Shaw cursed again, but he wasn't looking at the dead body. He was looking around the room. "Someone might have planted a bug in here. That's how the gunman could have known that it'd be a good time to strike while I was in the bathroom."

Sabrina started to search as well, but she had no idea what to look for. It sickened her to think that the second gunman could still be listening to all of this. Heck, he might have even heard of Shaw's plan to take her to headquarters.

"What's wrong?" she heard Shaw ask. But he didn't just ask. He hurried to her.

Sabrina realized then that she had her hand splayed over her belly. The pain was no longer mild. The contractions were harder.

"I'm not sure," she answered. She wanted to dismiss it, to say it would all go away. But she couldn't. Oh, God.

Was there something wrong with her baby?

There couldn't be. This couldn't be happening. Not after all they'd managed to survive.

"Hold on," Shaw warned her a split second before he scooped her up in his arms and stormed toward the door. What he didn't do was holster his gun. He kept it gripped in his hand as if he expected there might be another attack.

"Get me a cruiser, a car, anything!" Shaw ordered the uniformed officer. "And back me up because I'm taking Sabrina to the hospital."

Chapter Seven

This nightmare just wouldn't end.

Shaw scrubbed his hand over his face and mumbled another prayer. The baby had to be okay.

So far, everything had gone well at the clinic where the doctor had told Shaw to bring Sabrina when he'd made a frantic call to her after carrying Sabrina out of the hotel. But they were far from out of the woods.

"You know the drill," Dr. Claire Nicholson said to Sabrina as the doctor helped her onto the small padded bed next to the ultrasound machine. This particular room was just up the hall from the doctor's office, so they hadn't had to leave the building to have the procedure done. Thankfully, Sabrina had even managed to get a bite to eat while they were waiting for the room to be prepared.

Sabrina apparently did know the drill. She used a drab green cotton sheet to cover the lower part of her body, and she lifted her gown to expose her belly. Dr. Nicholson took a bottle of some kind of clear goo and smeared it over the exposed skin.

"Should I leave?" Shaw asked, hitching his thumb to the door where the doctor had entered just seconds earlier.

The doctor looked at Sabrina for the answer.

"Stay," Sabrina said. "Please."

She was scared. Shaw could see that in her pale color and constant lip nibbling. Hell, the doctor looked worried, too. He certainly was. So, he stood there, praying that this test would show that the baby was all right.

"How are the contractions?" the doctor asked Sabrina.

"Gone. Well, almost. I get Braxton Hicks every now and then, but they aren't at regular intervals." She paused, swallowed hard. "They are Braxton Hicks, right? I'm not in labor?"

The doctor began to move the tiny probe over Sabrina's gel-coated belly. "You don't appear to be. And you certainly haven't dilated. That's the first thing I checked when I examined you after Captain Tolbert brought you in."

Yes, Shaw had definitely waited outside for

that part of the exam. It had seemed to take hours, but he figured it was less than fifteen minutes before Dr. Nicolson had come out and said that the preliminary results were good, that Sabrina wasn't in the full throes of premature labor. But the doctor had still wanted to do an ultrasound before she declared the baby safe and sound.

"If all checks out well here, will Sabrina be able to leave?" Shaw asked. Because if the doctor planned to admit her to the hospital, that would require some serious security arrangements. The San Antonio Maternity Hospital was closed and being processed as a massive crime scene, and the other nearby hospitals had had to absorb the patients.

"I think under the circumstances, a hospital might be more stressful, and unnecessary," Dr. Nicholson concluded. "These false labors are fairly common in the last trimester. I seriously doubt the recent events had anything to do with it."

Maybe, but still Shaw didn't intend to let Sabrina out of his sight. Which, of course, would cause a whole set of problems of their own.

"We don't know why some women have false labor," the doctor continued, talking to Sabrina now. "But understand that it isn't your fault. Just relax and try to lead as normal a life as possible. That includes sex if…" She shrugged. "Well, if that applies to you two. I know Sabrina is a surrogate, but I sense something more going on between you two. Or maybe the potential for something more."

Shaw didn't look at Sabrina.

Sabrina didn't look at him.

"Forgive me if this sounds like a medical lecture," the doctor went on, "but recent studies show that sex, specifically a woman's climax, doesn't trigger premature labor. If the labor's going to start, it will with or without an orgasm."

Sheez. Shaw was trying to remember the last time he'd felt this uncomfortable.

"Oh, and sex doesn't hurt the baby, either, in case you were wondering," the doctor mumbled, and stared at the screen.

"Shaw and I aren't having sex," Sabrina interrupted. "Never have."

She seemed to imply *never will*.

"Right," the doctor added. She moved the monitor around. "The heartbeat's still good."

Finally, she was changing the subject. And it was a good change. Shaw stared, too, and saw the baby's images appear on the screen.

Oh, man.

He hadn't expected it to be so clear. He could actually see a baby.

His baby.

Shaw moved closer. Too close. His thigh bumped right into Sabrina's hand. Her fingers brushed against his fly, giving him an uncomfortable jolt.

"Sorry," he grumbled, easing back just slightly. But he couldn't take his eyes off the baby.

"The baby's sucking its thumb," the doctor said, and she chuckled.

Shaw couldn't believe it. "They do that in there?"

"They do a lot of things in there," Dr. Nicholson confirmed.

Sabrina chuckled, too. "In the last ultrasound, she was grabbing her toes. Between that and the daily soccer practice, she knows how to keep herself amused."

It nearly took Shaw's breath away. Seeing that would have been a miracle, and here he'd missed it because he hadn't come to the appointments.

Where the hell had his head been for the past eight months?

But he knew the answer. His head had been in the only place that his heart would allow it to be. With Fay. Her death was a wound that would not heal.

"You still want me to stay mum about the baby's sex?" the doctor asked. "Or do you want to know?"

Shaw looked at Sabrina. No more lip nibbling or signs of fear. She was smiling, and it was dazzling. Man, she was attractive no matter what the circumstances, but with that smile, she was drop-dead gorgeous.

And pregnant, he reminded himself, when he felt that damn tug of attraction.

Sabrina's eyebrow lifted just a fraction. She was obviously waiting for an answer as to whether he wanted to know if they would soon have a son or a daughter.

Too bad he didn't know what to say. "I'll get back to you on that, okay?" He hated that he sounded so removed from this. So angry. Hated even more all the conflicting feelings that were slamming into him at once.

What was wrong with him?

He could certainly go about bonding with this child without bonding with the mother. But that wasn't happening. Every minute he spent with Sabrina, he felt further removed from Fay. And he couldn't let go of her. He couldn't just forget all that had happened. Because if he did that...

He'd have to forgive Sabrina.

And himself.

He didn't deserve forgiveness. Here, all the months he'd blamed Sabrina, but the truth was that the blame was squarely on his own shoulders. His wife had been suicidal, and he hadn't realized it.

He hadn't stopped her.

"I have to go," he heard himself say. He went to the door, with part of him yelling at himself to turn around and accept what was on that examining table: Sabrina and his baby.

But he couldn't.

Shaw walked out and closed the door between them.

SABRINA FOLLOWED SHAW through SAPD Headquarters. She lagged a few steps behind him, on purpose, because she didn't want to look at him just yet.

The passing officers glanced at them. Probably because they knew of the latest attempt to kidnap her. Their glances could have also had something to do with the fact that she was wearing a loaner sundress from the doctor that was bright red and much too tight.

Of course, the glances could have been

because she was hurdling silent daggers at Shaw.

She was riled to the core. And hurt. They were a month away from being parents, and he was still shutting her out. She'd expected it, of course, but for some reason it hurt more now than it had weeks ago. Maybe because she thought that she and Shaw had developed some kind of weird camaraderie after running for their lives and fighting off hired killers.

Apparently, she'd thought wrong.

He opened the door to a room that was across the hall from his office. "It isn't much," he mumbled, and he ushered her inside.

Shaw was certainly right. It wasn't much. It was a small room crammed with two sets of bunk beds, a coffee table, a sofa, a tiny fridge, microwave on a metal stand and an adjoining bathroom that was equally sparse. A toilet, sink and tub equipped with a shower head attached to the wall. There were no windows, and the only light came from the florescent fixture overhead, which was humming.

"The guys call this the flop room," he explained. "It comes in handy sometimes when you've pulled back-to-back shifts and are too tired to drive home. Don't worry. I had them change the sheets and put in some fresh towels."

Sabrina settled for a "Hmm" and walked past him. She made sure no part of her touched any part of him. Unlike at the doctor's office where she'd gotten a cheap thrill from their accidental contact.

Shaw shut the door. "You can stay here until I've made other arrangements."

"This is fine," she practically snapped. But it was more than fine. It was safe. Well, hopefully. There was still that issue of a possible leak in the department.

"The door has a lock," he added, probably sensing her concern about that leak and security in general. To prove it, he flipped the switch, and she heard the click. "And you won't ever be in here alone. I'll stay with you until I can arrange for something safer."

Ironic, because this should be the safest place on earth. However, with a gunman still on the loose, no place was without risks.

She stood there. He stood there. And the silence closed in around them. Sabrina had never noticed before just how unnerving quiet could be.

"I'm sorry," Shaw finally said.

"Don't," she immediately answered. She started to walk away, but he caught her arm and eased her back around.

"I shouldn't have left you in the ultrasound room," he added.

She shook off his grip so she could fold her arms over her chest, and she stared at him, waiting for a more thorough explanation.

It didn't come.

"You have to learn to put this baby first," Sabrina clarified. "You hate me because I didn't talk Fay into giving up her dreams for a baby so she could stay alive. Yep, I got that. You've made it perfectly clear, but I'm sick and tired of you using that hatred as an excuse not to love this child." She unfolded her arms and aimed her index finger at him. "If this is the way you intend to act after she's born, then by God, I won't share custody with you. I won't expose this innocent little baby to all this negativity."

There. She'd wanted to say that to him for weeks. But now that she had said it, Sabrina instantly regretted it. She regretted it even more when Shaw looked as if she'd slapped him.

"I love this baby," he said, his words slow and deliberate. "And I don't hate you."

Confused, she shook her head. "You don't have to lie about your feelings for me. As long as you love the child, that's enough—"

"I don't hate you," he repeated.

Sabrina was about to challenge that again, but he took her by the arm and pulled her to him. In the same motion, before she could even catch her breath, his mouth went to hers.

And he kissed her.

He actually kissed her!

The jolt of surprise was instant. But there was another jolt, too. His mouth was gentle. The kiss, clever. With just the right amount of pressure to please her, and make her want more. It was a sensation that went all the way from her mouth to the center of her body.

He slid his hand around the back of her neck and eased her even closer. As close as her pregnant stomach would allow them to get. He angled her head, controlling her completely, and deepened the kiss. His tongue touched hers, and that jolt went through her again.

He made a sound deep within his throat. Not a sound of confusion. But of pleasure. It was all male. And totally designed to make her respond in the most basic female kind of way.

She felt herself go all damp, her body obviously preparing for something it'd wanted for a long time.

Shaw.

Specifically, Shaw naked and inside her. Sabrina no longer felt hugely pregnant and awkward. She felt she could fly as long as Shaw was there to fly along with her.

He slid his hand down her back. So slowly. His fingers caressed her along the way, lighting new fires wherever he touched. Not that she needed more. She was already too hot as it was. But Shaw managed to up the heat by cupping her bottom and adjusting their positions so that his sex actually managed to touch hers.

Sabrina nearly lost it right there.

It'd been so long since she'd been touched intimately that she felt close to a climax. And all from a simple touch and kiss.

Shaw took his mouth from her. But he didn't move the rest of his body. He stayed there, touching her and driving her crazy.

"I don't hate you," he repeated, his voice as strained as the muscles in his jaw. "I want to…" He kissed her again, and it was as hard as his sex was against her. "I want to, well, let me just settle for saying I want to have sex with you."

Sabrina didn't know who looked more surprised, him or her. "Really?" And she proved her shock by repeating that one word several times. "I figured I look disgusting to you."

"You look amazing," he corrected. He slid his thumb over her bottom lip, collecting the moisture that had gathered there from the kiss. He put his thumb to his mouth and ran his tongue over it. "You taste amazing."

But then he groaned, shook his head and stepped back.

Despite the loss of him touching her, the fire stayed with her, because she had a very good view of his incredible body, including that bulge behind the zipper of his pants. Sabrina was hot enough to want to ask if she could help him take care of that. She didn't know how. She hadn't experienced the logistics of pregnancy sex, but she was betting they could figure out a way.

"You had contractions earlier," he reminded her. "I shouldn't have kissed you."

"It was false labor," she reminded him, "and yes, you should have kissed me."

The corner of his mouth lifted. Almost a smile. Before he got serious again. "We have a lot to work out. Because I'm a man and because I want you, a certain part of me is suggesting we can work it out on that bunk bed."

Sabrina smiled, too. Then she got serious, as well. "But?"

"But while sex would be a good release,

it won't help us." He cursed and mumbled something about *I can't believe I just said that.* "I need to work out what's going on in my head before I work out what's going on in my pants. Understand?"

"Yes, I do." And Sabrina was being honest. A hot sexual attraction didn't mean they had gotten beyond the past. But maybe it was a start.

"Plus, I have to keep you safe. That has to be my priority. If I have you on that bed, safety won't be on my mind."

"Well, I should hope not," she said because she thought they could use a lighter moment.

He stared at her and reached out, as if he were about to pull her into another round of kissing. But there was a knock at the door.

"Captain Shaw, it's Officer Newell. I need to speak to you."

Newell, again. He certainly got around. And the thought of that made her uncomfortable. Sabrina shook it off and blamed it on paranoia. Being under attack had made her not want to trust anyone. Except Shaw, of course. She had no trouble trusting him. Or falling hard for him.

That kiss and these close quarters were going to complicate things beyond belief.

Shaw wiped his mouth with the back of his hand, took a deep breath and opened the door. "What is it?"

But Newell looked past Shaw and at Sabrina. "Gavin Cunningham is here at headquarters. Says he hired you and your company, Rootsfind, to locate someone for him. He's demanding to see you now."

"Good," Shaw informed him. "Because I want to see him. He obviously didn't commit suicide and wasn't murdered."

"No. But he is creating a scene."

"Where is he?" Sabrina asked. She walked closer to the door, but Shaw grabbed her to ease her behind him.

"You should be resting," he reminded her.

"And I will. But we both know this conversation could be critical. Gavin said he was responsible for me being taken hostage, and I want to know why he believes that."

"I can question him," Shaw insisted.

She gave him a flat look. "I'm betting you won't get far with him."

"He did say he wouldn't talk to anyone but her," Newell interjected.

Shaw still didn't seem ready to budge, so Sabrina added, "I can sit down while I talk to him. And if I can get him to confess any part he might have had in all of this, then you can arrest him."

It took several more moments before Shaw finally nodded, and they followed Newell down the hall and into another wing of the building. She found Gavin pacing in an interrogation room.

He was just as she'd last seen him, dressed to perfection in a tailored suit. His blond hair was perfectly groomed, as well. He looked the part of a young and upcoming attorney at the prestigious law firm where he worked.

Sabrina had run a background check on him after his first call to her, and she'd learned that even though he had been an attorney for only two years, he appeared to have a solid future and was well on his way to earning a seven-figure income.

"You're here," Gavin said. He didn't try to come any closer, but without taking his eyes off her, he slowly sank into the chair on the opposite side of the table from where Shaw and she stood.

Shaw had her sit as well, but he stood and glared at Gavin.

"For the record, this is being recorded." Shaw pointed to the camera mounted in the corner. "You have a problem with that?"

Gavin gave the camera wary look and then

shrugged. "No problem with it. I want the truth to be heard."

"Then we want the same thing," Shaw assured him. "So, why are you responsible for Sabrina being taken hostage?"

Gavin fired some uncomfortable glances among Shaw, Sabrina and the camera before his gaze settled on her. "I guess I should tell you this in front of him. After all, the police will have to get involved."

"The police are already involved," Shaw warned. "*I'm* involved. Now, start talking. Did you arrange for the women to be taken hostage?"

"God, no." He couldn't have sounded more outraged, but it was short-lived. Gavin huffed out several bursts of air and continued, "But I think I know who did. I think it was Wilson Rouse."

Now, that was a name she recognized. "The wealthy businessman who owns a chain of family style restaurants?" Sabrina clarified.

"The very one. I believe he might be my biological father. That's what I wanted you to try to confirm by using your resources at Rootsfind. I figured you had all kinds of databases and such that you could tap into and get me quick results. And by the way, he knows I'm here talking to you because I called him before I came over. I want all our dirty little secrets out in the open."

When Gavin didn't continue, Shaw made an impatient circling motion with his finger. "Keep going."

Gavin cleared his throat. "My mother died when I was six and never told me the identity of my father, but I recently found a letter where she mentioned Wilson Rouse. She implied they had an affair at the very time I would have been conceived. He was married and successful. Already a pillar in the conservative community. She was a waitress in one of his restaurants. So, I believe he dumped her when he found out she was pregnant."

"What does this have to do with the hostages?" Sabrina asked.

"Maybe everything. I wanted proof that Rouse was my father, so day before yesterday, I arranged to meet him by telling him I represented a potential investor. We met over coffee, and I confronted him. He denied everything and said he'd never fathered any bastard children. So, after he left, I took the cup he'd used and gave it to the lab tech at the San Antonio Maternity Hospital. I also gave him a sample of my DNA so he could compare the two."

So, that's how the DNA file had gotten there. Well, that was one mystery solved.

"Why take the DNA samples to the hospital?" Shaw asked.

"The lab tech was an old friend, and I thought he'd keep this between him and me. He didn't." Gavin closed his eyes a moment. "He called me before he ran the test and said even if the results didn't match, he could fake them, and that way we could get hush money from Rouse." He paused again. "Rouse wouldn't want his squeaky clean image tarnished. I told the tech, no blackmail, but I believe he called Rouse anyway and threatened him with the DNA tests he was running for me."

"So, what are you saying?" Shaw pressed. "That Wilson Rouse set up the hostage incident so he'd have a cover for his DNA and yours to be stolen?"

"That's exactly what I'm saying. Was the DNA stolen?" Gavin challenged.

Sabrina thought of the deleted file. Yes, it was possible that it had been.

Shaw didn't answer Gavin's question but went with one of his own. "What's the tech's name who had the sample?"

"Edward Reyes."

"The one who was killed early in the hostage standoff," Shaw provided.

Oh, mercy. So, the one person who could have cleared this up was dead. But they might finally have a motive for why this had happened. Of course, something still didn't make sense. If the DNA had been destroyed, then why would Wilson Rouse still want to kidnap her?

Sabrina had a lot of questions and doubts about what Gavin had just told them, but why would he lie?

Shaw turned and went to the door. He motioned for someone, and a moment later, Newell appeared.

"Two things," Shaw said, his voice low. Sabrina got up so she could hear what he was about to tell the officer. "What's the status of that list of people who knew about the hotel arrangements for Sabrina and me?"

"I'm working on it." Newell dodged Shaw's gaze and looked at Gavin. "Learn anything from him?"

"Yeah. That's the second thing I need. I have to speak to Wilson Rouse. Call him and get him down here. If he won't come, arrest him.".

"No need for that. He showed up about five minutes ago because he said Cunningham called him," Newell said, tipping his head to Gavin. "Mr. Rouse is waiting in your office. Should I bring him down here?"

"Absolutely. And get me that list. Within the hour, I want to know the names of everyone who might have put Sabrina and my baby in danger."

Newell walked away. Shaw glanced at Sabrina. Then at Gavin, and he motioned for Sabrina to step into the hall with him. He closed the interrogation room door.

"What's wrong?" she asked and went on the defensive. "Please don't say you don't want me here when you question Wilson Rouse because I want to hear what he has to say. If he's responsible for what happened to me, I have to know."

"So do I. You can stay." He looked down the hall where Newell had exited. "But for now, we might have another problem."

She followed his gaze. "Newell?"

"He couldn't look me in the eye."

Sabrina thought about the uncomfortable feeling she'd had about him showing up at the hotel the way he had. "You think he might be the leak?"

Shaw shook his head. "I don't know, but it appears as if someone compromised our location. A cop would be in the best position to do that."

"But Newell is the one who killed the gunman," she pointed out.

"Maybe to keep him quiet," Shaw pointed out just as quickly. He took out his phone and punched in some numbers.

"Who are you calling?"

"Someone I trust. Lieutenant O'Malley," he said to the person he'd called. "I know you're swamped in Homicide, but I really need a favor. A *quiet* favor. Run a check on Keith Newell for me. Dig deep and look for anything suspicious. *Anything.* And I also need you to see who would have known that Sabrina and I were in that hotel where we were attacked."

Sabrina couldn't hear what the lieutenant said, but his response was short and caused Shaw to nod approvingly.

"Yes, actually there is something else I need. Food and toiletries for Sabrina. I might have to keep her in the flop room for the rest of the day. Thanks," Shaw said a moment later, and ended the call.

He touched her arm with his fingers and rubbed gently. "Don't worry. I'll get to the bottom of this."

He would, if he could, but Shaw wasn't

a superhero, and the danger was still there, stronger than ever.

"Captain Tolbert," someone called out.

She recognized the tall man with the graying blond hair who was making his way toward them because she had seen his photo in the newspaper. It was Wilson Rouse. Apparently, round two was about to start.

Rouse walked closer. "Could we talk in private?" he asked Shaw.

Shaw shook his head and stepped just a few feet away. "No. This is Sabrina Carr, one of the maternity hostages, and she's in my protective custody. Wherever I go, she goes with me, so private conversations are out."

"Sabrina Carr," the man repeated. She didn't think it was her imagination that he had some disdain for her. "Gavin Cunningham came to you, and you encouraged his lies."

"Hardly." Sabrina lifted her shoulder. "Gavin just filled us in on the details. Before now, I had no idea that the biological father he wanted me to find was you."

"It isn't me. And whatever that slick weasel told you, it's a lie."

"Really?" Shaw said with skepticism dripping from his voice.

"Really. Because he's trying to set me up. You want to know who's responsible for that hostage mess?" He pulled out a small tape recorder from his pocket. "Well, I got the proof of who's guilty right here."

Chapter Eight

Shaw was having second and third thoughts about Sabrina sitting in on this meeting with Rouse and Gavin. He didn't want her more stressed than she already was.

But he also didn't want her out of his sight.

He trusted almost all his men, but those same men he trusted were swamped with the hostage investigation and the normal cases. Besides, it was possible that Gavin would be more open if Sabrina were in the room, and that openness could maybe lead them to the truth—even if this wasn't standard procedure to have a victim in the same room with the possible perpetrators.

"I want you to stay off your feet," Shaw insisted, and he led Sabrina back to the chair in the interview room where she'd sat earlier.

Shaw sat next to her, directly across from Gavin, but Rouse didn't sit. He walked in, slammed the door shut and aimed glares at all of them. He saved the more intense glare for Gavin.

"I have proof of what you've done," Rouse accused the other man.

"And if you hadn't stolen the DNA from the hospital lab, I would have had proof that you're my father," Gavin accused right back.

"Not a chance. I had your mother checked out, and she might have worked for me, but I didn't play under the sheets with the waitresses. Or with any woman other than my wife," he quickly added.

Rouse held up the miniature tape recorder and clicked the play button. Shaw immediately heard a man's voice.

An angry man.

"I won't let you get away with this, Rouse. So help me, I will make you pay. I'll ruin the only thing you seem to give a damn about— your precious name—and I don't care what I have to do to make that happen."

It was clear that it was Gavin's voice, and the young man jumped to his feet. "That conversation had nothing to do with what happened at the hospital."

Rouse smiled. "Didn't it?"

"You know it didn't. Play the rest of it." But then he shook his head and sank back down into the chair. "Yes, I did threaten him, and it'll sound as if I'm trying to set him up. But I didn't."

Gavin's reaction seemed honest, but Shaw wasn't about to declare him innocent of anything. "Why did you want to make Rouse pay?" Shaw asked. But he thought he already knew the answer—because Rouse wouldn't acknowledge that Gavin was his son.

"Tell him," Rouse prompted when Gavin didn't answer.

Gavin took his time responding. "I sued him on behalf of a client, and I lost."

"He lost because he tried to cut some corners with depositions, and I caught him in the act. It was his first big case," Rouse happily provided. "And he blew it big-time. That didn't sit well with the partners in his law firm, and since one of them is a golfing buddy of mine, I explained he should rethink his decision about keeping on the boy genius here."

Shaw silently groaned. He glanced at Sabrina, who had her eyes tipped to the ceiling. "So, you faked this whole fatherhood accusation to get back at him?" Sabrina asked Gavin.

"No!" Gavin practically shouted.

"You bet he did," Rouse contradicted, his

voice booming over Gavin's. "You have no blood of mine in your body. And you're not getting a penny of my money." He turned to Shaw. "My theory is that genius here decided to get his lab tech friend to help blackmail me. When that didn't work, he hired the gunmen, probably also friends of his, to make it look as if I wanted to steal my DNA."

Shaw shook his head. "That's a lot of trouble to go through to set you up because you tried to get him fired. People died during that hostage standoff. A baby is missing."

"Well, I'm not responsible," Rouse insisted, jamming his thumb to his chest. "Things probably got out of hand, especially if those gunmen were friends of his. They probably just panicked and screwed up."

"I didn't do this!" Gavin shouted.

The two men launched into a loud argument that could probably have gone on for hours, so Shaw stood and put an end to it. "There's one way to settle this. Both of you give me DNA samples, and we'll see who's telling the truth."

Well, the truth about fatherhood anyway. And it might be a start to the truth about why the hostages had been taken, if Rouse was truly Gavin's father.

"You want my DNA sample?" Rouse asked,

but he didn't wait for Shaw to answer. "Then get a court order. Oh, and good luck with that. Unlike the incompetent legal eagle here, I have an outstanding team of lawyers who'll fight you every step of the way."

"Thanks," Shaw said sarcastically. He reached out and took the tape recorder. "Now I can confiscate this. As potential evidence in a quadruple murder investigation."

"Keep it. Use it to put that weasel behind bars." Rouse flashed a dry smile at Gavin and walked out.

"I'll give you a DNA sample," Gavin volunteered.

Again, that seemed to imply he was innocent, but without Rouse's DNA for comparison, it was an empty gesture. Still, Shaw wouldn't turn it down. It would come in handy if they managed to get Rouse's.

"Go to the dispatcher at the front desk. He or she will make arrangements for a DNA swab," Shaw told him. He helped Sabrina to her feet. "In the meantime, I'll see about getting the court order for Rouse's sample."

"Do that, because he's my father, and I want him to pay for what he's done."

Shaw left Gavin still fuming in the interview room, and he led Sabrina back toward the flop room. "You think either Rouse or Gavin could be behind this?" she asked.

"Maybe. But I keep going back to that third deleted file. Taking your DNA test, I understand. Maybe things went wrong, and the gunmen decided you'd make a good hostage to cover their tracks. I can even understand Rouse wanting his DNA file deleted to protect his name. Or Gavin deleting it to make Rouse look guilty. But then what was in that third file?"

Sabrina made a sound of agreement. "Will your computer techs be able to recover it?"

"They're trying. I got an update while we were at the clinic, and I found out that there'd been two recent attempts to break into that lab at the hospital. That's the reason the new security camera was installed. The head of security had also changed the codes to access the DNA storage room."

"Yes. That makes sense. The gunman, not Burney Monroe, but the other one, he was furious when he couldn't open the door. That's when he shot the med tech. And then he shot the lock on the door. That's how he got inside."

So, maybe the Gavin or Rouse theory was right. If the dead med tech had agreed to help either of them, for a price, of course, he would have been a loose end. That could have been the reason he was killed so early on in the standoff. The gunmen no longer had any use for him. That meant Shaw needed to look for a connection between the gunmen and the lab tech.

Shaw opened the flop room and looked around, just to make sure there was no gunman or rogue cop lurking around and ready to attack. After the incident in the hotel, it would be a long time before he stopped looking over his shoulder.

"Sir, here's the takeout you ordered," someone said from behind him. It was one of O'Malley's men, someone Shaw trusted. Otherwise, he wouldn't have taken the bag and handed it to Sabrina. "I figured you'd need to eat something," Shaw told her.

She thanked him, Shaw gave the officer some money, and he closed the door and locked it. The toiletries he'd requested were there as well, sitting in a plastic grocery bag. There was even a change of clothes stacked next to the bag. Lieutenant O'Malley certainly worked fast.

"Eat," Shaw insisted. "And then get some rest."

She tipped her head toward the bathroom. "I think I'd like a shower first."

He nodded. The shower might help her relax, and it would give him a few minutes to get some much needed updates about the case. But Sabrina didn't head to the bathroom. She turned, stepped closer and looked up at him.

"I know I've been saying this a lot, but thank you. I'm not sure I would have gotten through this without you."

"You would have." But Shaw was glad he'd been there. For the baby's sake.

Sabrina's sake, too, he reluctantly admitted.

She leaned into him, putting her head against his shoulder. Like the other times they'd touched, he felt the attraction. The heat simmering between them. But he felt something else, too.

An intimacy that went beyond the attraction.

Again, he wanted to think this was all about the baby, but it scared him to realize it wasn't.

"What am I doing?" he asked, aloud. He'd meant to keep that question inside his brain, but it somehow made it to his mouth.

Sabrina pulled back, studied his face and then gave a heavy sigh. "I ask myself that all the time. I want you, too much," she added with a grimace. "But you're Fay's husband."

"Widower," he corrected, and he hoped that would sink in if he said it often enough.

"Widower." Sabrina repeated it, as well. When her gaze met his again, there were tears in her eyes. "You know what Fay said to me right before she died?"

He knew, though it hurt too much to remember. Fay had phoned Sabrina, after she'd taken a bottle of sleeping pills, and Shaw knew this because it'd been Sabrina who had contacted him, had told him to get to Fay, that she was dying. Shaw had listened to the message that Fay had left on Sabrina's answering machine. It'd been part of the routine investigation to declare Fay's death a suicide.

"We don't have to talk about this," he insisted.

But Sabrina continued as if she hadn't heard him, "Fay told me to take care of you. I swear, I tried to do that."

She had. That's what this baby was all about. At least, it'd started that way. It felt different now. *He* felt different. But the guilt was still there.

"Do you know what Fay said to me when she was in my arms dying?" he asked. Part of him wondered why he was opening this too-raw wound, and the other part knew it had to be done.

Sabrina blinked back tears and shook her head.

"Fay said I should take care of you, that you and I should have the baby that she couldn't give me."

The breath rushed out of her, and Shaw held her because she looked ready to fall. "I'm sorry. So sorry," Sabrina repeated. "I didn't know she said that. She shouldn't have asked that of you."

"Yeah. She should have. Fay had a lot of problems. Old baggage from being abused in her childhood. New baggage from the infertility issues. But she always put me first. Even when she was dying, she knew how important a baby was to me. How much I wanted a family of my own."

That was his old baggage. He hadn't been adopted like Sabrina or abused like Fay, but his parents had been killed in a car accident when he was five years old. He'd been shifted around from one family member to another, never finding a place he could call home.

Yeah, the old baggage had shaped him, too.

Shaw had to take a deep breath. "If I hadn't

wanted a child so much, then Fay might be alive today."

Sabrina frantically shook her head. "She desperately wanted a baby, too. You're not at fault here. Fay's depression is what killed her."

"You're not at fault, either," he whispered. He reached out and wiped away the tear that was sliding down her cheek.

She stood there, staring at him and blinked. "Did we just have the air clearing that we'd been avoiding?"

"Yeah. I think we did." And it felt good. Not perfect. But good. Shaw certainly didn't think this would take away the guilt. It would always be there.

But the question was, just how was it going to affect what he was starting to feel for Sabrina?

"Time for that shower," she mumbled, and grabbed the bag of toiletries and stack of clean clothes from the table. She walked toward the bathroom, leaving him to deal with that question he might never be able to answer.

"If you don't mind, I'll leave the door open just a fraction," she called out to him. "That way, I can hear you if you call. Or if I call you. I might have a little trouble getting out of the tub."

That got his attention. "You need help?" And yeah, it sounded a little sexual, but he was serious. He didn't want her falling.

"I should be fine, and I promise if you have to come running to haul me out, I'll cover myself with the towel. I wasn't kidding about those stretch marks."

She grinned and adjusted the door so there was about a two-inch gap.

Shaw smiled as well and then cursed because this wasn't the time to be cheerful. Maybe he'd get a chance to do that when Sabrina and the baby were safe.

He heard her turn on the shower and about a minute later, he caught just a glimpse of a very naked Sabrina stepping into the tub. She slid the shower curtain so that it shielded her, but not completely. He could still see her outline behind the vinyl.

Oh, man.

The raunchy thoughts started, and here only minutes earlier, he'd been a somber widower. Now, he felt more like a sex-starved teenager.

Because he had to do something, anything, to get his mind off her, he rifled through the takeout bag, took one of the three sandwiches—turkey on wheat—and started to eat. He also forced his eyes away from Sabrina's nude silhouette. Thankfully, he got a little help in the distraction area because his phone buzzed.

"Lieutenant O'Malley," Shaw answered after he saw the officer's name on the ID screen.

"I don't have much info for you, but I figured you'd be anxious for an update."

"I am." He was anxious for a lot of things, including the woman behind the shower curtain. Shaw forced his attention to stay on the conversation. "What did you learn?"

"Still no word on that third file that was deleted, but we've accessed the hospital's online storage. The company that manages it is going through the cache of old files and comparing them to what's in the system now. We might get lucky and find out what was deleted."

"Good, that's a start. What about the officers who might have known where Sabrina and I were staying?"

"Newell's on the list of those who knew, along with about a dozen others in Special Investigations. The location was kept in the department, but we're still looking at hotel employees. One of them could have tipped off the gunmen."

True. Shaw had minimized how much time Sabrina was in the lobby and in front of the hotel, but it was still possible that someone had recognized her. After all, the hostages' photos had been all over the news.

"I'm still running the background check on Newell," O'Malley continued. "Nothing immediately sticks out, but I'm getting his financials."

Another good start. "Any idea why he was at the hotel this morning?"

"None. He was off duty, but he does seem obsessed with this investigation. About a year ago, he had a case with a hostage, and it didn't end well. The hostage was killed. Maybe that's all there is to it—he's trying to right an old wrong."

After what he'd been through with Fay, Shaw understood that, but he wasn't about to trust Newell just yet.

"Keep digging," Shaw insisted.

"I will, and I might soon have an update on the evidence we're processing both from the hospital and the hotel room where Burney Monroe was shot and killed. CSI and Trace are working nonstop, and the reports are coming in."

Maybe there'd be something in all that evidence that would break this case wide open.

"I had a conversation with Wilson Rouse and Gavin Cunningham in interview room

2B," Shaw told the lieutenant. "Could you have someone look at the disk? It was recorded. What I need is for someone to review it and get me a court order for Rouse's DNA."

O'Malley hesitated. "That won't be easy."

"No," Shaw agreed. "But it might provide us with a motive. I also want a tail put on Gavin Cunningham. He's probably still in the building giving us some of his own DNA. After you see the interview, you'll know why all of this might turn out to be critical."

"It sounds it. Anything else?"

Shaw went through his long, mental to-do list. "Any word on the second gunman?"

"Not yet. He's still at large."

Yeah. And as long as he was, then Sabrina wouldn't be safe. "Any leads?"

"Maybe. Burney Monroe was a low level computer tech for a supply company. That might have been why he was hired to do this particular job. He definitely had the computer hacking skills. He also has a younger brother, Danny. He has no phone and no listed place of residence, but he works as a data entry clerk, also low level, and his boss said he's due on shift at midnight."

Shaw jumped right on that. "Did this brother miss work during the time of the hostage incident?"

"He wasn't on the schedule so the boss doesn't know where he was. Still, he said Danny's a good worker, and he never had any problems with him."

"But Burney could have talked him into this." Or someone else.

"True," the lieutenant agreed. "If the two learned about Sabrina and you, maybe they thought they could use it somehow. Maybe to gain money, maybe to gain some kind of legal favors?"

Yes. Because the bottom line was that Rouse and Gavin might simply be distractions. This whole mess could have been orchestrated by the two gunmen, Burney Monroe and his partner. And if they found the partner, they might learn there was no need for Rouse, Gavin and their collective DNA.

Still, he couldn't discount that it was Gavin's DNA file that had been deleted and the sample stolen.

"One more thing," Shaw continued. He checked first to make sure Sabrina was still in the shower. She was, and with the water running she wouldn't be able to hear this. "Have someone run a check on Dr. Claire Nicholson, Sabrina's OB."

O'Malley made a sound of surprise. "You think she might be involved in this?"

"Probably not. But I keep going back to the fact that the gunmen stole Sabrina's DNA. I want to know who told them to do that, and why."

"You think it's connected to you, because you're her baby's father?"

"Could be. When the gunmen took her from the hospital, Sabrina overhead them say they were going to use her to get me to cooperate."

"Well, that could be motive. But a lot of people already knew the child was yours. Newell certainly knew because I heard him talking about whether or not to collect money to buy a baby gift."

Hell. So, they were back to square one— still suspecting Newell but knowing that this could all be circumstantial.

"I'll put together a team I trust to start handling this," O'Malley let him know. "And, Captain, hang in there. We'll get this SOB even if he's one of our own."

Shaw hoped that was true. A dirty cop wasn't always easy to catch. But neither was a dirty community leader or a lawyer.

And speaking of cops... "How's Bo Duggan?" Shaw asked.

O'Malley wasn't quick to answer. Shaw understood. O'Malley was married, the father of three, and he was no doubt thinking of his own wife and family. "Bo's trying to deal with it. It's not easy. Plus, he's got newborn twins to take care of."

That would have been more than enough on one man's plate, but now Bo had to bury his wife. "Make sure Bo gets as much time off as he needs."

"I will."

He thanked the lieutenant and hung up just as Sabrina turned off the shower. Shaw knew it wouldn't be long before she came back into the room, so he quickly composed himself. There wasn't anything he could do to help Nadine Duggan, but he sure as hell could find the people who'd contributed to her death and put them behind bars.

The shower curtain rattled back, and he got up in case she needed help. Just seeing her helped with the blue mood, and he wondered when the hell Sabrina had become his lifeline to getting through this.

Right.

It'd happened when he started lusting after her.

Yeah, he watched her and told himself it was because he wanted to make sure she didn't fall. That was a huge part of it, but that didn't justify the cheap thrill of seeing her naked. He didn't see any stretch marks, probably because he was gawking at her breasts. They were full and looked ready for the taking.

His taking.

He groaned, looked away and walked closer to the door. "You okay?"

"Yes, other than having no clean panties. There weren't any in the stack of clothes. But I'm washing the ones I have and hanging them on the towel rack. As thin as they are, they'll be dry in no time."

There was the sound of more water running, some moving around sounds, and several minutes later, the door fully opened. Sabrina stood there in a loose blue dress the color of the Texas sky on a good day. Barefooted. Her wavy, long auburn hair was damp and clung to her neck and the shoulders of the dress.

She looked and smelled like Christmas and his birthday all rolled into one.

"Did you just admit you're not wearing panties?" he asked. He meant it as a joke, but the joke didn't quite come through in his voice.

The need did, though.

"It was meant as a warning, so you wouldn't be shocked when you see them dangling from the towel rack." Her expression was light, too, but he didn't miss the long, lingering look she gave him.

"You need to eat," he reminded her. And himself. He stepped to the side so she could get past him. "There are some sandwiches, apples, juice and milk."

Sheez, he sounded like a waiter and decided to shut up.

He couldn't turn off his eyes, though. Shaw watched her cross the room. She was light on her feet for being eight months pregnant.

"Join me," she insisted. She took the bag from the table and took it to the sofa, probably because it was more comfortable than the metal chairs at the small table in the kitchen area.

He did join her, after taking a deep breath.

She opened the plastic bottle of milk, took a sip and stared at him from over the top of the bottle.

The air was suddenly scalding hot.

Still, Shaw took his partially eaten turkey sandwich from the table and sat next to her on the sofa. He was hungry. His stomach was growling, but food didn't seem to be his body's top priority.

Sabrina lowered the bottle and licked the

milk from her lips. She probably hadn't meant for it to be provocative, but it was.

Hell, at this point her breathing was provocative because it pushed her breasts against the front of her dress.

"What are you thinking?" she asked. She set the milk on the coffee table.

He started to lie, to tell her he was thinking about the investigation. But it would have been such a big lie that it probably would have gotten stuck in his throat.

So, no lie.

Just the truth. And he'd show her what he was thinking.

Shaw tossed his sandwich onto the table, reached out, clasped the back of her neck and hauled her to him. He caught her slight sound of surprise with a kiss.

Oh, he was going to regret this.

He knew it. Sabrina knew it.

But that didn't stop him.

He kissed her, hard, and pulled her onto his lap.

Chapter Nine

Sabrina didn't have time to think. Nor did she want to. The only thing she wanted was Shaw, and apparently she was going to get him.

Finally!

Judging from the heat of the kiss, he didn't intend to stop.

She certainly didn't intend to, either. Sabrina went willingly when Shaw moved her onto his lap. Her belly prevented them from having full body contact, but it didn't stop the fiery kiss that Shaw was delivering.

The fire wasn't just in his kiss. It slid right through her, from her mouth all the way to the part of her that wasn't covered with panties. She got an interesting reminder of that when she felt Shaw's thigh press against her there. Mercy. Here she was again. Barely a touch, and she was ready to have him inside her.

Shaw didn't make a move to unzip his pants and give her what she wanted. Instead, his mouth left hers and went to her neck. He dropped a flurry of kisses around her jaw. On her throat. But when the kissing exploration made it to the base of her ear, Sabrina moaned. He took the cue and gave her a French kiss there that had her moaning for more.

More was difficult to get.

She tried to wiggle closer to him, so that his sex would touch hers, so she could finally have some relief from this burning ache that was too hot to control. But again, her belly got in the way.

Shaw stopped the neck kisses and pulled back so they were eye to eye. For one horrible moment, she thought he was going to say this had to stop. She thought he was going to move away from her.

That didn't happen.

Sabrina sat there, waiting, with her breath gusting and her heart racing out of control.

"Shh," he said. His voice was soothing and slow.

So was his hand. He slid it from her neck to her breasts. And he circled her right nipple with his fingertips while he watched her.

Sabrina had no choice but to watch him as well, even though that touch caused her to moan again, and her eyelids fluttered, threatening to close.

"Shh," he repeated. His hand went lower, sliding against her, and creating little fires wherever his fingers touched.

He stopped for just a moment when his hand reached her thigh, and with the fire blazing in his blue eyes, he pushed up her dress.

His gaze never wavered. He remained focused on her face. And his fingers trailed up her thigh. Then, over.

To just the right place.

The pleasure speared through her. Instant. Hot. Intense. So intense she had to close her eyes, and she angled her hips forward so that his clever fingers would go deeper inside her. They did, and with a few of those well-placed strokes, he had her right at the edge.

Sabrina forced her eyes open, and she shook her head, questioning him. They should do this together, with his sex inside her.

But Shaw shook his head as well, and he leaned forward to kiss her. It was French. And perfect. The kiss from a man who knew exactly what he was doing. And what he was doing was taking her to that edge.

Alone.

Sabrina wanted to fight it. She wanted to pull back and coax him into joining her. But the kiss continued, hard and deep. So did those maddening strokes with his fingers. Each one, faster.

Harder.

Deeper.

Until she couldn't fight the sensations. She couldn't hang on. Her body betrayed her, and she felt the climax ripple through her.

She slumped forward, because she had no choice, but Shaw caught her and buried his face against her neck. They stayed there, pressed together, until Sabrina could gather enough breath and strength to pull back.

The corner of his mouth lifted. Then lowered just as quickly when he apparently saw her expression. "Oh, no. We're not going to have that argument."

Maybe it was the post-climactic fog in her head, but she wasn't sure what he meant. "Argument?"

"The one where you try to convince me that we should have full-blown sex. Or some other form of pleasure that will end in me having what you just had."

Sabrina blinked. Yes, that was the argument she had been about to launch. She decided instead to get her point across without words. He was hard and huge behind his zipper, so she pressed her hand against him.

A hoarse groan rumbled in his throat, and

he moved her hand away. "Tempting, but it can't happen. I need to think, and I can't think if we're having sex."

"We could make it fast." And she was only partly joking. She was still punchy from the climax. "I just want to make you feel the way I'm feeling."

"I am," he assured her. It didn't seem like a lie, either. He leaned in and brushed a kiss on her mouth. Then, he eased her off his lap. "Watching you was incredible."

It didn't feel incredible. Sabrina suddenly felt a little awkward. She'd never had sex that particular way, and Sabrina didn't like the idea of her getting something that Shaw was denying himself.

"Don't overanalyze it," he mumbled. "This wasn't about pity. It wasn't about all the old bad feelings between us. I just wanted to watch you."

How could she argue with that?

Besides, she was too mellowed out with the aftershocks still humming through her. And she didn't want to argue. There had already been too many disagreements between her and Shaw to add another one.

"Now eat," he insisted. He got up and walked to the bathroom. "Then, rest."

Sabrina fixed her dress, pulling it back

down in place. She fixed her position, too, and moved so she was sitting rather than leaning into the space where Shaw would hopefully soon return. Then, maybe they could talk.

Or not.

Sabrina thought about that. They were light-years ahead of where they'd been just days earlier, and it was probably best if she didn't push things.

He's Fay's husband.

That old label flashed through her head again, and she felt the guilt return. Oh, mercy. When was this going to stop?

"You okay?" Shaw asked.

She glanced up to find him staring at her. "I'm fine," she insisted.

He looked as if he might challenge that, but he didn't. He came back to the sofa and started in on the sandwich that he'd discarded prior to their make out session. He took exactly one bite before his phone buzzed.

Shaw pulled out his cell from his pocket, glanced at the screen and answered it. "Lieutenant O'Malley."

The officer he trusted. Sabrina only hoped he was trustworthy and good at his job. They needed information.

She ate while Shaw listened. She couldn't hear what the lieutenant was saying, but judging from Shaw's suddenly intense expression, this was an important call.

"Where's the baby now?" Shaw asked.

She remembered there was a missing newborn. Shaw had said an Amber Alert had been issued. Maybe this call was to tell him the child had been found. She prayed that was the case anyway. Even after all the hell she'd been through, having her baby disappear would be much, much worse.

"I want that umbilical cord tested ASAP," Shaw continued before he started another long round of listening.

The minutes crawled by, punctuated only by Shaw's occasional question.

"Repeat that," he said. And his expression tightened even more. "No. You go ahead and question him. I think it's safe to say that it'd be a conflict of interest for me to do it. Record the interview, of course. I want to hear every word."

Shaw ended the call, slipped his phone back into his pocket and blew out a long breath.

Sabrina had so many questions, but she started with the obvious one. "You found the missing baby who was taken from the hospital?"

"No. This is a different baby, one not involved with the hostages." He shrugged.

"Well, maybe it is. We just don't know at this point. The tech guys were able to retrieve the deleted file and were able to match it to a DNA request that was generated right here in SAPD four days ago."

Just three days before they were all taken hostage. The timing was certainly suspicious. "Whose DNA?"

"The missing baby's. His birth mother was missing as well, but then her body was found. She was murdered. And the baby wasn't with her. None of her friends and relatives know where the child is, but a family member stated that the dead woman had had some problems with the baby's birth father. He'd made threats about taking the child."

"And the father's name?" Sabrina asked.

Shaw shook his head. "We don't know. Neither did the family member because the dead woman had kept the relationship a secret. That's why the DNA test was ordered. The birth mother had had the baby's cord blood stored at the hospital, so we were able to get a good sample to try to identify the father. Because obviously the father is a murder suspect."

Oh, mercy. Another murder. Another missing suspect. Except this might be the same person who'd created all this havoc. "Will the techs be able to recreate the missing file?"

"No. It had been corrupted, probably on purpose. And the baby's cord blood was missing from the hospital storage room." Shaw paused. "This might be the motive for why the hostage situation happened."

Of course. A birth father who didn't want his identity known because he'd murdered the mother of his child. Sabrina prayed he hadn't done the same to the baby.

She eased her hand over her own child and gave him a reassuring rub. "How will you find this monster?"

"We have several ways. We're trying to track down the dead gunman's brother, Danny Monroe. It's possible he was the second masked gunman who took the hostages. Or he at least might know if his brother was the baby's father."

"Or he could have just been the hired gun," Sabrina pointed out.

Shaw nodded, looked at her. He smoothed his fingers over her bunched up forehead. "Don't worry."

"Right." She nearly laughed. "I want this person identified and found so that our baby will be safe."

"I want the same thing," he assured her. He sat there with his own forehead bunched up.

"There's more," she said. "What?"

"Two things." But then he paused again. "I'm having your OB, Dr. Nicholson, checked out. It's just routine," he added quickly. "She had access to your medical records, and I want to make sure she didn't leak that info to anyone." His eyes came to hers. "Did you know that she'd once been romantically involved with Officer Keith Newell?"

"No." Sabrina took a moment to let the surprise settle in. "But then she doesn't talk about her personal life. How involved were they?"

"Involved. They've known each other since high school. Turns out he listed her as one of his references when he applied to the police academy."

Sabrina gave that some thought, as well. She also thought of how supportive the doctor had been. "That doesn't mean Dr. Nicholson has done anything wrong."

"No. It doesn't." Shaw shook his head, cursed under his breath. "But the report I just got from O'Malley could point the guilty finger right at one of my own men."

Chapter Ten

Shaw stood in the shower and let the scalding hot water spray over him. It didn't help unknot the muscles in his back. Probably nothing would except for an arrest.

Thankfully, that might happen soon.

Not so thankfully, he might have to arrest a cop.

Lieutenant O'Malley had gotten back Newell's financials, and there was an unexplained ten thousand dollars that had been deposited into his account the day before the hostage incident. Ten grand wasn't a fortune by some people's standards, but it was a lot to a cop. And it was a red flag since there weren't any other similar deposits over the last few years. It also didn't help that the money had been transferred into his account from an offshore bank.

Shaw was still waiting to hear Newell's

explanation, and by God, it'd better be a good one.

He bracketed his hands against the tiled wall and leaned into the shower spray so it'd hit the back of his neck. He didn't stay in that position long. He couldn't. He needed to finish up and get back into the flop room with Sabrina.

She'd been asleep when he turned on the shower. And the flop room door was locked from the inside. Newell was in Lieutenant O'Malley's office and would stay there until the lieutenant got some answers. So, Newell wasn't running around the building, ready to strike, but Shaw didn't want to leave Sabrina alone too long.

He dressed in the jeans and black T-shirt he'd had brought to him from his locker. They weren't exactly his normal work clothes, but they'd have to do for now. He didn't have time to drop by his house and pick up his usual dark pants and dress shirt.

Shaw quickly brushed his teeth and used his hand to comb his hair. He opened the door, ready to tiptoe back into the room, but Sabrina was there, standing right in front of him, dressed in the paper-thin gown that'd been among the loaner clothes. Her dress was tucked beneath her arm.

"Anything new on Newell?" Sabrina immediately asked.

Shaw shook his head. "Lieutenant O'Malley said he would call as soon as he got to the bottom of this."

She grumbled something under her breath and pushed her hair away from her face. "I fell asleep," she said as if that were the last thing she wanted to do. "Did you?"

"I napped on and off throughout the night." But it felt as if he hadn't slept for days.

She lightly touched her fingers to the bruise above his eye. The injury he'd gotten when Burney Monroe bashed him in the head with his gun. "It's turning purple." The corner of her mouth lifted. "The color goes well with your eyes."

He wanted to smile, wanted to share this softer moment with her, but he glanced down at the bruises on her wrist. Burney Monroe was responsible for those, too.

Sabrina must have noticed where he had his attention because she shifted the dress, hiding her hands beneath it. "I'm fine," she assured him. "Well, other than having to use the bathroom."

"Oh." He stepped out of the way, but not before brushing against her. As usual, his body started to beg for something it wasn't going to get.

Not now, anyway.

It wasn't a matter of *if* sex with Sabrina would happen, it was now a matter of *when*. It was amazing how much forty-eight hours could change things.

While Sabrina was in the bathroom, Shaw decided to go ahead and call O'Malley. Yes, the lieutenant might be at a crucial point in his interview with Newell, but Shaw didn't want to wait any longer.

"I was about to call you," O'Malley said the moment he answered Shaw's call. "I just finished up with Newell and need to head home for a while so I can take a nap, wash up and change my clothes. Nadine Duggan's memorial service is today. But I can talk while I'm walking to my car."

Nadine. Shaw mentally groaned. He would have liked to go to the service, to pay his respects and give Bo some support, but it was too risky to take Sabrina out like that.

"Where's Newell right now?" Shaw wanted to know.

"He's on his way to the memorial service, too. Or at least that's where he said he was going. I couldn't hold him, Shaw. He said the money came from online poker winnings.

Of course, the poker site is offshore and not exactly eager to cooperate with the police in San Antonio. Still, Newell was able to go to the Web site where he won the money."

"But he couldn't prove the money was a poker payout?"

"Not exactly. He showed me a screen name, and that person had indeed won a large sum of money, but I can't be sure Newell and the winner are one and the same. But I haven't given up yet. I'm still working with the poker site to release the financials. In the meantime, I have a uniformed officer tailing Newell."

Good. The uniform would remind Newell that he was under investigation, and the cop could report back any suspicious activity. But that didn't make Shaw feel any better about Sabrina.

"I need a safe place for Sabrina to stay for a while," Shaw explained. "And after what happened in the hotel, I'd rather not use anything put in place by Special Investigations. Newell probably has a lot of buddies in the department who might not understand he could be a dangerous man."

"I have an idea. A good friend owns an apartment on the Riverwalk, and he's out of town. I've been keeping an eye on the place for him, but it's yours if you want to use it."

"Thanks. I'll take you up on that." It would get Sabrina out of headquarters so that she wouldn't run into Newell. It would also free up the flop room. Shaw had dozens of officers pulling double shifts, and he didn't want to tie up the room any longer, especially when there was a safer alternative.

"The address is six-eight-eight Commerce, apartment four-C. I'll put the key in an envelope and leave it with the motor pool dispatcher. You can get it on your way out. Good luck, Captain. Call me if you need me."

Shaw jotted down the address and checked his watch. It was barely 5:00 a.m. and still dark outside. Probably a good time to move Sabrina to the apartment. Shaw was about to tell her that when she stepped from the bathroom, but she spoke before he could say anything.

"You have to feel this." She had a big grin on her face when she walked to him, and she took his hand and plopped it on her belly. She no longer wore the gown. She had on the blue dress she'd worn the day before.

He immediately felt the kicks. Unlike the last time, however, these were nonstop.

"The baby's boxing this morning," she joked.

Shaw leaned down so he could press his

ear to those thumps. He couldn't hear them, but he could still feel them. "I think she needs some breakfast."

"She can hear you, you know. So, if there's anything you want to say to her…"

Shaw looked up at her, and his eyebrow slid up. "She can hear me?"

"It's true. I read nursery rhymes to her."

Shaw got a clear image of Sabrina doing just that. While she was wearing that flimsy gown that showed off her breasts. But then, he thought of another image. His baby had heard those gunmen. The shots. All the violence.

And that riled him to the core.

No baby, especially his baby, should have that kind of start in life.

"Hang in there," he whispered against Sabrina's belly. "Daddy's not going to let anything bad happen to you, sweetheart. Promise."

He looked up at Sabrina again, but her smile had faded. Her eyes were shiny as if she were about to cry. "Do you think she's really a she? Or is it a boy?"

He thought about the offer the doctor had made to tell them the baby's sex. "Honestly, it doesn't matter." And it didn't. "The baby's gender has never been part of this dream family I have in my head. I'd be happy with either. I just want him or her to be healthy."

Her eyes watered even more, and Shaw decided to put a stop to that.

"You need to get your things together," he instructed. "We're moving to a safer place this morning."

She nodded, blinked hard and turned to start collecting her toiletries. Shaw was about to help her, but his cell buzzed. It wasn't O'Malley but another of his lieutenants, Joe Rico. Yet someone else Shaw trusted.

"Captain Tolbert, one of my men just brought in Danny Monroe. I thought you'd like to know."

"Danny Monroe," Shaw mumbled. The brother of the man who'd tried to kill him and kidnap Sabrina. Oh, yeah, Shaw wanted to know about this. "Where is he?"

"I had him taken to the interview room just up the hall from you. I also have a preliminary report on him that my lead investigator just handed me. I thought you'd like to see it. I also thought you'd want to be the one to question him."

"You bet I do." But he glanced at Sabrina. He didn't want to leave her alone in the flop room, so she'd have to come with him. "I'll be there in a minute."

"They found Danny Monroe?" Sabrina asked the moment he hung up.

"They did, and I'm about to question him. Are you up to being in the same room with him?"

"Absolutely."

She seemed certain enough, but Shaw wasn't so sure. He didn't want to create more stress for her, so he'd keep the interview short and let Lieutenant Rico dig into the details.

If there were any details to dig into, that is.

He waited for Sabrina to slip on her sandals, and they walked up the hall. Not far. Just a few steps, and he saw Lieutenant Rico waiting outside the interview door. The lieutenant handed Shaw the preliminary report he'd mentioned.

"There's nothing in the report we can use to hold him," Rico explained. "But he doesn't have a solid alibi for the hostage incident. He claims he was at his apartment, sick with the flu."

Shaw glanced through the report. First the biographical details and then the criminal record. Danny had one, all right. Breaking and entering when he was a juvenile. As an adult, there was a drug charge, but he'd pled down and was on parole for two years. There were others, including an assault in a bar fight and resisting arrest.

But the common denominator in all the incidents was that Danny had been with his older brother, Burney.

"Thanks," Shaw told the lieutenant. He left Rico outside and led Sabrina into the room.

Shaw noticed the resemblance right away. Danny was a younger version of the dead man Shaw had seen lying on the floor of the hotel room.

"You're the cop who killed Burney?" Danny immediately accused.

Danny had been sitting behind the metal desk but jumped to his feet. He was visibly upset, with the veins bulging in his neck, and Shaw whispered for Sabrina to stay near the door. He wanted to get her out of the room fast if there was any sign of trouble.

"No. Another police officer shot your brother while he was committing a felony. He tried to kill me, and he tried to kidnap Ms. Carr." Shaw tipped his head to Sabrina.

"So says you."

"So says me and Ms. Carr and the other officer who witnessed it. Burney broke down the door to a hotel room and fired a shot at me." And those were all the details Shaw intended to give him. "Now, where were you yesterday morning and the afternoon before?"

"I already told that other cop—I was home sick in bed." He coughed as if to prove his point.

Shaw wasn't ready to buy the cough or the story. "I don't suppose you have anyone who can verify that?"

"Just Burney. He called me on my cell night before last, right about the time you cops say he was holding all those women hostages."

"Good. Then we can use phone records to verify that." He cracked open the door and asked Lieutenant Rico to run the phone records immediately.

Danny only shrugged. "I could be mistaken. Maybe it wasn't night before last when he called. Maybe it was some other time. Maybe he didn't call me on my cell after all. Like I said, I was sick and in bed. I could have dreamed it."

"Don't worry. Lieutenant Rico will get it straight. He'll learn when your brother called and where he was when any calls were made." Shaw made sure it sounded like a threat, because it was.

Danny opened his mouth. Closed it. Then, opened it again. "Look, I don't want you trying to pin anything on me. I already have to deal with my brother's death, and I don't need you guys breathing down my neck."

"If you're innocent, you have nothing to worry about." Shaw sat down across from him. "Talk to me about your brother. Why would Burney want to take those women hostage?"

"Who said he did?" Danny fired back.

"For argument's sake, let's say he did. Why would he have done that?"

Danny shrugged again and began to fidget with a hangnail on his right thumb. "I don't know. All I know is I had nothing to do with any of this."

Shaw pushed harder. "Then guess why Burney would have gotten involved in a hostage situation."

The fidgeting continued. "It might have had something to do with an old friend who called him last week out of the blue."

Now this sounded promising. "This old friend got a name?"

Danny swallowed hard. "Gavin Cunningham."

Sabrina made a soft gasp. Shaw did some mental cursing. He didn't like that Gavin's name kept coming up in this investigation.

"Keep talking," Shaw ordered.

"Gavin wanted Burney to help him prove

the identity of his birth father. Gavin was all worked up about it, said it was really important."

"Did he say why?"

The fidgeting moved from his thumb to his jaw. Danny scrubbed his hand over his day-old stubble. "He didn't say, but Burney thought it might have something to do with money. I mean, it's usually about money, isn't it?"

Not always.

And especially not in this case.

Did Gavin and Burney conspire to tamper with the DNA so it wouldn't prove that the missing child was Gavin's and therefore connect him to the murder of the baby's mother?

Or was there something else going on here?

"I didn't have anything to do with those hostages or with what happened yesterday when you say Burney tried to kill you," Danny insisted. He looked Shaw straight in the eye. "And I think it's time for me to call a lawyer. I know my rights, and that means this chat session is over. If you want to hold me here, you have to arrest me."

Shaw considered it, especially since Danny would perhaps call Gavin. After all Gavin was an attorney, and he wouldn't mind seeing how the men interacted. Still, he didn't have enough to hold Danny.

But that didn't mean he couldn't have Danny followed.

Danny didn't wait for Shaw's approval. He hurried out ahead of them and rushed down the hall. Shaw made a call to dispatch to request that a tail be placed on the possible suspect. Maybe, just maybe, Danny would go to the person responsible for all of this.

Shaw caught Sabrina's arm so he could lead her back into the corridor where Lieutenant Rico was waiting. The lieutenant was holding some papers that had been stapled together.

"These are Burney Monroe's phone records," Rico announced. "We'd already started to run them before Danny Monroe came in." The lieutenant wasn't smiling, but it was close.

Sabrina glanced at the records, then back to the lieutenant. "Please tell me those records put Burney on the fourth floor of the hospital when I was being held hostage."

"Not quite. He probably used a prepaid cell when he was there. He had one in his pocket when he was killed, but it was brand-new. My guess is he threw the old one away just in case he was caught. These records are from his regular cell phone, the one he has an account for."

So, no giant smoking gun.

"But there is a call from Burney to Gavin Cunningham," Rico explained. "He made it three days before the hostages were taken. And the call lasted nearly an hour."

"Interesting," Shaw mumbled.

"Yeah, but not as interesting as these." Rico pointed to the three calls that had been highlighted. They were all the same number.

"Who did Burney call three times?" Shaw wanted to know.

The lieutenant smiled. "One of the richest men in the city, and the very person Gavin Cunningham claims is his father. Wilson Rouse."

Shaw gave that some thought and then handed Rico back the phone records. It wasn't proof of Rouse's guilt, or Gavin's for that matter, but maybe this could finally bring things to a head.

If Shaw bent the truth a little.

And for Sabrina and his baby's safety, he would bend the truth. He would do whatever it took.

"Use this to get a court order for a sample of Rouse's DNA," he instructed Lieutenant Rico. "I want it compared to Gavin's, just in case that connection turns out to be relevant to this investigation. And then I want you to do one more thing."

Shaw paused, gathered his thoughts and fine-tuned how this could work.

"I want it leaked that we've found some DNA from the missing baby whose mother was murdered," Shaw continued. "Say that we got the DNA from the baby's pacifier that we found near the crime scene, and we've been able to extract enough to do a DNA comparison so we can identify the birth father."

"Comparison to whom?" Rico wanted to know.

"To Wilson Rouse, Gavin Cunningham, Danny Monroe, his brother and Officer Keith Newell. Leak it that whichever one is the father, he'll be arrested for capital murder and about a dozen other charges."

Rico nodded, then paused. "You do know how to stir up a hornet's nest, Captain."

Yeah. Now, Shaw only hoped he and Sabrina weren't the ones who got stung.

Chapter Eleven

Sabrina followed Shaw through the maze of corridors that, according to the signs, led to the parking garage.

She was actually thankful to be on their way out of headquarters because it'd taken nearly three hours for Shaw to tie up some details about the shooting and the hostage investigation before they could finally leave. There'd been one call after another. Several reports to be read. Questions that couldn't wait for answers.

Shaw had taken all those calls, read the reports and listened to the updates while they were in the flop room, again. It hadn't been easy for her to sit there and wait. Waiting only gave her too much time to think about the danger.

"You think Rouse will fight the DNA court order?" she asked as they walked.

"Of course. He won't want his good name

linked to any of this, but the more he fights, the more it's linked. I'm hoping that will spur him to confess what took place in those three conversations he had with a dead gunman."

She hugged her spare clothes and the plastic bag of toiletries to her chest. "Could he have hired Burney Monroe to steal the missing baby's DNA sample and delete the file?"

"Maybe." Shaw shook his head. "Rouse would certainly have had a lot to lose if this dead woman, Misty Martinez, had named him as her baby's father."

"Because it would confirm his extramarital affair?"

"There's that. But let's just say she wasn't exactly in his circle of friends. She was a cocktail waitress at a seedy bar downtown. From all accounts, she was beautiful but with some questionable habits. She also became a criminal informant after she was arrested for drug possession."

This wasn't painting a very pretty picture of the dead woman, but she still didn't deserve to be murdered. "When did you learn all this?"

He lifted his shoulder. "I had the report on her brought to me last night."

Which meant he hadn't gotten much sleep. Those naps he'd mentioned earlier had no doubt been very short with lots of work in between. Maybe when they got to this so-called safer place, she could prod him into resting the same way he'd been doing to her.

"This dead woman, Misty Martinez, was a police informant," Sabrina commented. "Did she also have a connection to Officer Newell?"

Shaw paused at the door that led to the parking garage and glanced around, probably to make sure no one was close enough to hear them. Sabrina checked, too. But she didn't see anyone within earshot.

"It's possible there's a connection," Shaw explained in a whisper. "She had some information about a hostage case that got botched last year. Newell was partly responsible for that botch."

The wild ideas started to fly through her head. "So, maybe Newell blamed her in some way and then killed her." But then she shook her head. "That really isn't much of a motive for murder and stealing a child."

"Unless Newell fathered the woman's baby. He wouldn't have a sterling reputation to tarnish like Rouse, but it wouldn't make him look good in the department's eyes if he was sleeping with a criminal informant."

True. But then, it probably wouldn't look

good to Gavin's high-end law partners, either. Of course, that left Sabrina wondering where was the baby now?

Shaw opened the door, and they went into the parking garage. He stopped by the dispatcher who was in a small cubbyhole office attached to the back of the main building, and retrieved an envelope. When he opened it and looked inside, she saw a key.

"It's for the place where we'll be staying," Shaw whispered to her. He put it inside his pocket.

He also got the keys for an unmarked car. Probably because he didn't want to use his own vehicle to drive to the new location. It was yet another security precaution that she hoped would pay off.

Shaw put his hand on the small of her back, and as quickly as she could move, he got them away from the dispatch office and into the open parking lot. He hurried toward a black four-door sedan that was in the center row, amid dozens of cars. Some were cruisers, some designated for SWAT and other special units, and there were other unmarked vehicles, as well.

He unlocked the car with the keypad, and threw open the door. Sabrina leaned down to get inside when she heard the sound.

A blast tore through the air.

It took her a moment to figure out what the sound was. It was so loud that it was like an explosion. But it wasn't.

Someone had fired a shot.

Shaw shoved her onto the passenger seat, and she dropped the clothes and toiletries onto the ground. In the same motion he drew his gun from his shoulder holster. His gaze rifled all around them. So did Sabrina's. But she couldn't see who'd fired that shot.

"Get in the car," Sabrina insisted. She was partly covered, but Shaw was literally out in the open.

He stayed put, still looking around, but he did crouch lower next to the seat where Sabrina had hunkered down.

"Captain Tolbert, did you fire that shot?" someone called out.

Sabrina peeked over the dash and saw the dispatcher peering out from the covered area. He, too, had his weapon drawn and ready.

"No," Shaw answered. "It wasn't me. Get a visual on the shooter."

The response had no sooner left his mouth when there was another blast. Sabrina hadn't seen where the first bullet had landed, but she saw this one because it tore into the top of the car door just inches above Shaw's head.

She grabbed him to pull him inside with her, but he shoved aside her attempt and dropped even lower to the ground. It still wasn't low enough.

He was a sitting duck.

The gunman fired again, and the bullet shattered the glass in the passenger-side door. Sabrina automatically shielded her eyes, but the safety glass stayed intact. However, another shot sent a chunk of that webbed glass dropping right onto Shaw.

"The shots are coming from the top of one of the buildings," Shaw shouted to the dispatcher.

Oh, mercy.

There were a lot of buildings around them. Headquarters was right in the middle of downtown, and there were tall office buildings and hotels on all four sides. They were surrounded, and the shooter could be up on top of one of them, ready to deliver the fatal blow.

But who was shooting?

She tried to imagine the person behind the trigger. Gavin? Rouse? Newell? Or maybe this was just another hired killer. Someone whose job it was to make sure she and Shaw didn't get out of this parking lot alive.

The next shot blasted through the car and

took out the back window. The bullet that followed gashed through the roof. Even though the sun hadn't fully risen, she could still see the light spearing through that slashed metal. It was a vivid reminder of just how little protection the car actually was.

Sabrina got onto the floor space between the dash and the seat. There wasn't much room, but she squeezed in somehow, and she put her hands over her belly in case those shots made it to her.

She was turned so she could still see Shaw, and she watched as he lifted his gun and fired a shot of his own. The blast was even louder, because he was so close, and she pressed her hands even harder over the baby to try to shelter her from the noise.

"He's up there," Shaw called out, pointing toward the building directly behind the car. He scrambled to the other side of the door, away from the gunman.

Good. At least Shaw was semi-protected now, and they knew where this monster was. That meant he could be stopped.

Well, hopefully.

Even though Sabrina couldn't see the building's exit, certainly other officers had responded by now. Maybe even someone with a rifle who would have the firing range to shoot the guy.

Shaw handed her the car keys through the broken window glass. "Without getting up, turn on the engine, put the car in gear and start driving forward. Only tap the accelerator with your hand to get it moving."

Sabrina shook her head. "No."

"Yes!" Shaw insisted, shouting over the next round of shots. "It doesn't matter if you can't see where you're going. When the car rolls forward and gets to the headquarters building, someone will tell you what to do. They'll pull you out and get you to safety."

That wasn't why she was shaking her head. "And you'll be out here in the open."

"Not for long. I'll run and get in front of one of the other cars."

And while he was doing that, he could be shot.

"Think of the baby," he reminded her.

It was a dirty way to get her to cooperate. But it was also an effective one. Sabrina desperately wanted to do something, anything, to keep Shaw safe, but she couldn't do that at the baby's expense.

Their child had to come first.

She could see Shaw through the crack in the open door. Well, she could see part of him, anyway. That was more than enough for her to see his resolute expression. He wouldn't back down on this.

"Do it," he ordered, his voice booming over the shout of the nonstop barrage of shots. Those shots were literally tearing the car apart.

When the shots made it to the dash, so close to her head, she knew she couldn't wait any longer.

"Stay safe," she told Shaw.

Sabrina reached up, shoved the key into the ignition and started the car. Somehow she managed to put it into drive. There was no need for her to touch the accelerator as Shaw had suggested because the car started to inch forward.

She caught just a glimpse of Shaw before he left the cover of the passenger door and started to run.

Oh, God.

The shots were nonstop. One loud blast after the other. It took her a moment to realize some of the shots were coming from headquarters. Someone was returning fire.

Sabrina couldn't tell if Shaw made it to the cover of another vehicle. She couldn't tell anything, other than that the car was indeed moving, and the gunman was continuing to shoot. She put her head against the seat, squeezing herself into as tight a ball as possible so if there was an impact, the baby wouldn't be hurt.

"Turn the steering wheel to the left," someone shouted. She recognized the voice. It was Lieutenant Rico, who'd talked to them earlier.

Sabrina did as he instructed.

"Turn it slightly to the right now," Rico added. Like Shaw, he had to shout over the sound of the gunfire. "You're almost here."

She waited for the impact of the car bumping into the building. But there wasn't one. Instead, she felt the car turn to the left, toward the covered area where the dispatcher's office was. And she soon realized why. There were two officers who had hold of her bumper and were guiding the vehicle. The moment the vehicle came to a stop, one of them pulled her from the car and hurried her inside.

There were at least a half dozen cops waiting there, and they didn't allow her to stay close to the door so she could see what was going on. A uniformed cop took her by the arm and put her in an interrogation room about twenty feet away.

"What's happening out there?" she asked him.

But he only shook his head and headed back to the door. "Stay put," he warned.

She did, because she didn't know what else to do. And she prayed while she heard the shots continue. God knew how close those shots were coming to Shaw. Maybe he'd even been hit, but that was too painful to even consider.

Sabrina counted off the seconds, hoping that each count would end the attack. Finally, the shots stopped. She could hear the shouts of officers barking out orders.

What she didn't hear was Shaw.

There was the sound of the dispatch office door opening, and Sabrina peered around the corner, hoping this was someone with good news.

It was Shaw.

And he had blood on his face and the front of his shirt.

Nothing could have held her back at that point. She hurried toward him, catching him in her arms. "You're hurt."

"Not much. Just nicks from the broken glass." He used his arm to wipe away some of the blood and sweat, and he pulled her closer to him. "Are you okay?"

"I'm fine," Sabrina lied.

She didn't have any physical injuries, but it

would take her a lifetime or two to forget those images of the bullets coming at them, and Shaw scrambling for his life across the parking lot. "What happened to the shooter?"

He brushed a kiss on her forehead and pulled back so he could look into her eyes. "He might be dead or at least injured. We think one of the sharpshooters from the SWAT was able to take him out because he stopped firing."

That sent her heart pounding again. "You *think?* You mean he could be getting away?" No. This couldn't continue. It had to stop.

"Shh," he whispered and pulled her to him again. "We have a team making their way to the top of the building. It shouldn't be long before we know for sure."

"And if he's not dead?" But Sabrina wasn't sure she wanted to hear the answer.

Especially when she heard another shot.

This one wasn't a thick blast as the others had been, but it still sounded close. "What's happening?" she asked.

Shaw shook his head. "My men will give me an update as soon as they safely can. Don't worry. If the gunman tries to escape, we already have officers assembled at the base of the building. He won't get away. If we can take him alive, even better. Because we might finally learn who's responsible for these attacks."

Sabrina clung to that hope. She also clung to Shaw. It was probably stupid to hand him her heart and well-being this way, but she couldn't stop herself. He'd just saved her life again. A real hero. And she was falling hard and fast for this particular hero.

His cell buzzed, and Shaw jerked it from his pocket. But it obviously wasn't a call he expected because he cursed under his breath.

"Newell," he greeted, but the greeting was more like a growl. He pressed the speaker phone button. "You picked an odd time to call."

"It's important. I want to know why you're having me followed."

"Now isn't a good time to talk."

"Why am I being followed?" Newell pressed.

Shaw took a deep breath. "Because you're under investigation."

Now, Newell cursed. "Because of those poker earnings I had deposited into my account."

"Among other things. Look, someone just fired a couple of dozen shots at Sabrina and me, and I don't have time for this conversation."

"Make time…*sir*." But Newell didn't say the title with much respect. "This is my career, and it's the most important thing in the world to me. I don't know what you think I did, but I'm innocent. I'm a good cop."

"Then the evidence will prove that." Shaw didn't give the officer a chance to say anything else because he hit the end call button.

The dispatch door flew open. Shaw turned, though he still stayed protectively in front of her. It was Lieutenant Rico who came walking toward them.

"We got him, Captain," Rico announced, looking straight at Shaw. "He's injured, but he's talking. And he wants to talk to you."

Chapter Twelve

Shaw didn't ask the identity of the wounded gunman. He had one goal—to get to the man while he was still alive so he could get some answers.

But he didn't want to do that unless Sabrina was safe.

"Stay with Lieutenant Rico," Shaw told her, knowing he'd get an argument, but he stopped it before it could start with a quick kiss.

Yes, it was a cheap shot, and Sabrina deserved better, but he didn't want to risk her going outside again until he was positive the area was safe. Right now, he wasn't positive of that at all.

Shaw peeled off the grip Sabrina had on his arm and hurried to the dispatch door. "I won't be long," he told her, but he wasn't sure that was true. He wanted to get as much from the shooter as he could and that might take a while.

He ran across the motor pool parking lot and out the side entrance where a uniformed officer was standing guard. There were lots of officers, just as Shaw expected, but the bulk of them were near the back of the building where he'd spotted the gunman. The guy had likely tried to escape using that route, and he'd been shot when he wouldn't surrender.

The sun was up now and already bearing down on him so he worked up a sweat by the time he made it to the crowd of officers. He pushed his way through, wondering just who he'd see lying on the ground.

Gavin, maybe. It could even be Wilson Rouse or someone he'd hired. It was possible Shaw might not recognize the assailant at all.

But he did.

The man was Danny Monroe.

Shaw cursed. He should have held the SOB even if it meant bending the law.

"Captain Tolbert," Danny said, his voice weak. It seemed he was trying to smirk. The front of his shirt was covered with blood, and even though Shaw could hear the ambulance sirens, the man didn't look as if he would last long.

"You wanted to talk to me," Shaw said, once he got his jaw unclenched. He wanted to finish Danny off for endangering Sabrina and the baby. The SOB didn't deserve to take even one more breath, but Shaw knew each breath could give them answers.

"Take notes," Shaw told one of the uniforms who immediately took out a notepad. One of the others took out a mini tape recorder and moved closer. Good. Shaw wanted every word of this taken down so it could be scrutinized.

"It wasn't personal," Danny said, looking right at Shaw. "This was cleanup for my brother. His debts got passed on to me, and I needed to pay them off or die."

"It felt personal," Shaw let him know.

"I figured it did. That's why I have to set things straight with you. I want you to go after who put this plan together. Go after the person who hired Burney, because if Burney hadn't needed the money so bad, he wouldn't have done this."

"Who hired him? I'll be glad to go after him." And Shaw didn't intend to show any mercy. Not to Danny, nor this idiot who'd put this plan together.

Danny shook his head and dragged his tongue over his bottom lip. "I don't know who's responsible. Burney just said we had to get in the hospital lab and get some DNA samples and destroy a file. It was supposed to be easy, but people kept getting in the way."

"What people?" Shaw demanded.

"We thought that woman, Bailey Hodges, had seen us trying to get in the lab the day before we took the hostages. She saw Burney trying to break the new lock, or at least we thought she had. So, we found out who she was. That's why Burney went after her. Burney had been warned not to leave any witnesses who could identify us."

Bailey. Sabrina had said the gunmen were calling out the woman's name. Now, he knew why. The gunmen wanted her dead. It was a good thing they hadn't found her.

Behind them, the ambulance screeched to a stop, and the medics rushed out with a gurney. Shaw knew he didn't have much time.

"Why were you and Burney supposed to get the DNA samples?" Shaw asked.

"I don't know. That's the truth. But the bastard who hired Burney will know. That's why you have to find him. You have to make him pay for killing us."

That didn't tug at any of Shaw's heart-strings. "Did you ever speak with the man or woman who hired you?"

"Just today for the first time. Burney handled all the other calls. The other details. I was told what to do. I had to pretend to be a nurse, Michael Frost, so I could call the women we needed to get to the hospital that day."

Well, that was another piece of the puzzle that had been solved.

"Whoever the boss is," Danny continued, "he was putting a lot of pressure on Burney. Burney owed money, you see, lots of it, and the loan shark was coming after him. That's why we got desperate and took the hostages so we could get everyone to back off and we could get into the lab. We did what we were supposed to do. We destroyed the DNA file… and took your woman."

Everything inside Shaw went still. A temporary reaction, no doubt, because he felt a strong storm brewing.

The medics moved between Shaw and Danny and began to get him ready to be transferred to the gurney.

"Whose idea was that, to take my *woman?*" Shaw demanded.

Danny shook his head again and drew in a ragged breath. "I don't know. Maybe Burney's. Maybe not. Burney thought if anything went wrong, then you'd make the cops back off if we had her."

Hell, he might have done just that. He

wouldn't have been able to sacrifice Sabrina and his baby. Not even for this investigation.

But that didn't mean the boss of this operation had been the one who ordered Sabrina to be taken.

"Were you trying to kidnap her again today?" Shaw asked as the medics hoisted Danny onto the gurney.

"I got a call from the boss, from the SOB I want you to find. He asked if I had a gun, and I told him I did. I keep a hunting rifle in the trunk of my car. So, he told me to get to the nearest rooftop and fire a lot of shots. Not fatal ones. The boss wants you both alive. This was just meant to scare you, to show you what could really happen if you don't cooperate. He was going to make that clear, he said, after you were good and scared."

So, there could still be more contact and more threats from the so-called boss. And that meant Shaw wasn't getting in the ambulance to ride with Danny to the hospital. He didn't dare leave Sabrina alone.

Shaw looked around at the group of officers and spotted Sergeant Harris McCoy, the hostage negotiator he'd worked with when Sabrina and the others had been taken.

"Go to the hospital with him," Shaw ordered. "Get as much from him as you can.

And make sure he's got a guard on him around the clock."

Not that Danny was likely to attempt an escape in his condition, but it was possible his boss would try to eliminate him before he could say too much.

"Yes, sir." Sergeant McCoy moved to the head of the gurney and started toward the ambulance.

Shaw waited until the ambulance drove away before he walked back to headquarters. It was a short distance but a long walk, and he knew what he had to tell Sabrina wouldn't do much to put her at ease. The danger was still there, and as long as it was, she had to remain in his protective custody. That was the official label for it anyway, but he didn't intend to let her out of his sight again.

Sabrina was waiting for him in the hall just on the other side of the dispatch door. Rico was there next to her, and he had his phone pressed to his ear. No doubt getting an update as to what had just happened.

"Lieutenant Rico said the shooter was Danny Monroe," Sabrina said, her voice shaking.

"He was. But he said he was just a hired gun and he couldn't or wouldn't finger his boss."

What little color she had drained from her face. "So, his boss could send someone else?"

"In theory. But that person won't be any more successful than Danny and his brother were." Shaw slipped his arm around her and looked at Rico. "I'm taking her away from this. Sergeant Harris is in the ambulance with Danny. When he finishes the interrogation, I want to know what the man said."

"Will do," Lieutenant Rico assured him. He moved closer to Shaw and lowered his voice. "You wanted the false info leaked that we'd found a pacifier from the missing baby and that we'd been able to extract DNA. I took care of that right after we talked. That would have been about two hours or more before the shooting started."

Two or more hours *before*. Maybe that hadn't been enough time for Danny's boss to have gotten the word and order the shooting. Unless the leak had been fast, like from someone in the department. Then, it was possible Newell could have called Danny and told him to fire those shots.

"Someone was supposed to be tailing Danny," Shaw remembered.

Rico nodded. "From what I can tell, Danny practically ran out of the building after he finished talking with you. By the time the dispatcher got someone assigned, Danny was already gone. The officer was on his way to Danny's place to look for him when the shots stared."

Again, Shaw hoped Danny hadn't been able to make a fast getaway because a cop had any part in this.

"I'll call you with an update as soon as I have one," Lieutenant Rico said, and he walked away.

Shaw stood there a moment, volleying glances between Sabrina's troubled eyes and the dispatch door. The last time he'd taken her out that particular route, Danny had fired shots at them. Danny had been adamant that he wasn't trying to kill them, which might be true, but any of those bullets could have ricocheted and hit Sabrina.

"Are we going back to the flop room?" she asked.

Despite the small size, it had its advantages. It was close and safe. Well, except for the fact that Newell might be behind this. He thought of the key to the apartment that O'Malley had offered him. Going there would get Sabrina away from Newell, maybe, but too much could happen between headquarters and the Riverwalk.

Shaw nodded. "Yeah. The flop room again. I'll arrange some food to be delivered since you didn't eat much of your breakfast earlier."

"And you should arrange for some medical attention. You have two new cuts on your face."

He swiped at them to see if they were still bleeding. They were. But since he wasn't gushing blood, he wasn't about to waste time seeing a medic.

They were only a few steps from the flop room when Shaw saw two people that he really didn't want to see right now. Gavin Cunningham and Wilson Rouse. They were scowling at each other and were being escorted by not one but two uniformed officers.

"They demanded to see you, sir," one of the officers said. "They got here a few minutes before the shooting started, and I had them wait in your office."

"Not a good idea," the other officer added. "They nearly got in a fight."

He was a popular man this morning. First, Danny. Now these two.

"You're bleeding," Gavin observed.

"Yeah, so I've been told. I was on my way to clean up, but I'm guessing you two think this is a good time to air some more dirty laundry."

"You bet it's a good time. Tolbert, what you're doing is harassment," Rouse challenged. Unlike Gavin, he didn't even seem to notice Shaw's cut face. "A court order for my DNA? I'm fighting it. It'll be a cold day in you-know-where before I voluntarily give you my DNA. Now, I hear rumors that you think I hired the clowns who took the maternity hostages."

"He did hire them," Gavin insisted.

Sabrina glanced at both men. "Did you two show up here together?" And there was a lot of impatience in her voice. She was probably as fed up with these two as he was. Especially since one of them might have hired Danny to fire those shots.

"No," Rouse and Gavin said in unison.

It was Gavin who continued. "I called him, to tell him I was coming here before I went in to work. I wanted to demand that you arrest him, to get him off the streets, and he decided to come, too."

"So I could stop him from pursuing that *demand*," Rouse snarled. With his eyes narrowed, he looked at Shaw. "You have nothing to connect me to this."

Shaw didn't want to do this now, but since

he had the opportunity, he decided to run with it. "Nothing except phone conversations with the dead gunmen who did take the hostages."

Gavin made a sound of triumph. Rouse, however, just looked puzzled.

"The dead man's name is Burney Monroe," Shaw supplied.

"Him." Rouse scowled. "Yes, he called a couple of times. And get this, he called to ask me for a loan, because he said he worked at one of my restaurants when he was a teenager and had now fallen on hard times. He said I owed him some back pay. I had my people check, and he never worked for me. I told him that, too, when he called me back."

Shaw glanced at Sabrina to see if she was buying any of this. She looked as skeptical as Shaw felt. And she looked as tired. It might be early morning, but it had already been a long day.

"He's lying," Gavin insisted, hitching his thumb in Rouse's direction. "Run his DNA, compare it to mine, and you'll see that he's my biological father. And he wanted to cover that up."

"Gavin has a point," Sabrina mumbled, directing her comment to Rouse. "If you quit fighting the court order for the DNA test, then this will all be cleared up. The test will prove you aren't Gavin's biological father…"

She stopped, and like Shaw she was studying Rouse's reaction.

"Unless you are his father," Sabrina finished.

"I'm not." Rouse's mouth twisted, relaxed and then twisted again. "But what the hell if I was? All that would prove is that thirty years ago, I was a stupid, weak man. That's all. It doesn't mean I committed a crime, and it doesn't mean I deserve to have my family's name dragged through the mud like this."

Gavin, Shaw and Sabrina all stared at Rouse.

"You're Gavin's father," Shaw concluded. This conversation had just taken a very interesting turn.

"That's what I've been saying all along," Gavin interjected. He didn't make that sound of triumph again, but it was in his eyes.

However, there was no triumph for Rouse. It seemed as if the fight had been taken right out of him. "I won't comply with that court order," he mumbled. He then turned and made his way past the uniforms and down the hall.

"You aren't going to arrest him?" Gavin asked. But his voice was practically a whisper.

Maybe he'd just realized that having a biological father wasn't the same as having a dad.

It was a lesson Shaw didn't want his own baby to have to learn.

"He's guilty," Gavin insisted, jabbing his index finger in the direction that Rouse had just exited. "If you want to keep Sabrina safe, then you'll put him behind bars."

Shaw had had enough of this. "When there's evidence to prove his guilt, or yours, that's when I'll make an arrest."

Gavin looked as if Shaw had slugged him. "My guilt? You think I've done something wrong?"

Shaw didn't answer. "Go to work, Gavin. Let us do our jobs, and I swear I will learn the truth. It's just a matter of time, and if that truth leads me to Rouse, then I'll personally arrest him."

Gavin stood there, staring, his eyes focused on the floor, his breathing uneven. "I just hope the truth doesn't come too late," he mumbled. Then Gavin, too, turned and left.

"Finally," Sabrina said, glancing at his face again. "Let's get to the flop room so I can clean those cuts."

They walked toward the flop room while he looked down at her stomach. "Any cramps?"

"None."

He hoped she was telling the truth, but he wouldn't put it past her to smooth over how she was really feeling just so there wouldn't be more pressure on him. But the pressure was already there. Sabrina and the baby were his top priority.

And he was afraid that didn't just apply to their safety.

He opened the flop room, and a detective who was lying on the sofa immediately got to his feet. "Captain. I was, uh, just taking a nap. Double shift."

Shaw nodded. "There's a sofa in my office. You can use that."

The detective nodded and didn't waste any time getting out of there. Shaw locked the door behind him.

Sabrina immediately headed for the bathroom, and she returned with a wet washcloth. "Sit," she instructed. She took him by the arm, positioned him on the sofa and sat next to him. "And then convince me why I shouldn't be calling a medic."

"Because I'd rather have you nurse me back to health." He tried to sound cocky, even tried to smile, but he couldn't when he saw her expression.

With her so close, he could see the emotion and the fear in her eyes. They'd come close to dying, again. Even though this was the third hellish event in just as many days, he knew it wasn't old hat. Never could be. That's why her hands were shaking.

She dabbed at the nicks, turned the washcloth to a clean spot and dabbed some more.

"How bad do I look?" he asked.

Shaw touched his fingers to her arm and rubbed gently, hoping it would soothe the raw nerves that were right at the surface. Her bottom lip was trembling now, and her eyes were shiny. Sabrina was on the verge of crying, but she was fighting it.

She pulled back the washcloth and stared at him. It seemed as if she wanted to say something. Probably not related to the nicks she was cleaning. No, this would be something far more important.

But then she shook her head.

"That bad?" Shaw said, still trying to keep things light.

Sabrina looked down at the cloth in her hands. "You're the most attractive man I've ever seen. A few cuts and a bruise won't change that."

Surprised and a little embarrassed by the unexpected compliment, he thought he might have blushed. He put his fingers under her chin and lifted it so they'd have eye contact.

"Shaw," she whispered the moment their gazes met.

He couldn't stand to see her like this, but he didn't have any idea how to make the fear go away. So, he did the first thing that came to mind. He leaned closer and put his mouth on hers. Shaw kept it soft. Gentle.

And, he hoped, reassuring.

While he was hoping, he added that she would agree to get the rest that he was about to suggest. Yes, it was still late morning, but the adrenaline crash was going to leave her bone tired. It was certainly playing a number on his own head and body. But instead of rest, he wanted to hold her. To have her hold him. He needed to believe all of this would turn out with both Sabrina and their baby safe.

She touched his face, keeping everything slow and gentle, and she eased him closer to deepen the contact of the kiss. Shaw continued to keep it reassuring.

Well, he tried.

His attempts went south in a hurry, though. Because Sabrina didn't just deepen the kiss. She touched her tongue to his and slid her hands from his face to his neck. To his chest. And his body went from being interested to being on fire.

Man, he wanted her more than his next breath.

Shaw shook his head, trying to fight through the haze and the heat. He considered pulling back. It was the smart, responsible thing to do. To pull back and insist she take a nap.

But he didn't.

He continued to kiss her. Continued to ease her closer and closer. Maneuvering her until he had her on his lap. The last time they'd been in this position, things had gotten intimate fast. Maybe too fast.

"Don't think," Sabrina warned.

Don't think?

He was about to laugh that off, but then she slid her hand from his chest to the front of his pants. The fire went to full blaze and was hotter than Texas heat.

Shaw took her advice and didn't think, other than to accept he would probably regret this.

Later.

Much later.

For now, he just went with the need to take Sabrina. She certainly went with it, as well. The intensity of the kissing went up a notch. So did the touching. And she had him seeing stars and cursing when she went after his zipper. Shaw very much intended for that zipper to go down, but he needed to gather a little control of the situation.

And himself.

His body was begging him to take her fast and hard, but his body wouldn't get its way on this. He forced himself to slow down. Not easy to do. Not with Sabrina kissing his neck and pressing herself to him. He wasn't helping much in that department, either, because he continued to kiss her as if his life depended on it.

Maybe it did.

That thought came from deep within, but he pushed it aside. Sabrina was right.

Now wasn't the time for thinking.

Since her dress was loose and stretchy, he shoved it up so he could get to her breasts. Evidently, both of them were past the point of foreplay, but Shaw intended to satisfy a few fantasies. He shoved down the cups of her lacy white bra and put his tongue to good use on her breasts.

She was full and warm. Like silk. But tasted like sin. Apparently, the breasts kisses were a fantasy for her, too, because she made a sound of pleasure that went straight through him. That sound was a primal invitation to take more.

So he did.

While he kissed her neck and that sensitive little spot just below her ear, he was rewarded with more of those silky moans. More pressure from her body against his. Until everything inside him was yelling for more.

Sabrina gave him more.

She caught on to her panties, hooking her fingers around the elastic band and peeling them off. It wasn't easy, and Shaw helped because suddenly getting her naked was the only thing that mattered. He pulled the dress off over her head and sent it flying across the back of the sofa.

He didn't stop. Didn't bother with finesse, though he swore he'd try better if he got this lucky again. Sabrina shoved down his zipper, jerking open his jeans so she could take him from his shorts.

Shaw took things from there.

He turned and dropped back onto the sofa, so that Sabrina was on top and straddling him. It was another fantasy fulfilled. Sabrina with her pregnant belly, her full breasts and that look of pure heat on her beautiful face.

She put her hands on his chest to steady herself and slid her fingers through his chest hair. She eased her hips forward. Slowly. Inch by inch.

Until she took him inside her.

The pleasure was instant. Intense. And Shaw had to close his eyes a moment just to absorb what was happening. Sabrina obviously had something to absorb, too, because she made that incredible sound of pleasure and slid her sex against his.

Shaw caught her hips to help with the

thrusts. Not that she needed help. She seemed to know exactly what she was doing and how to get both of them to a fast, hot climax.

Her belly prevented any mouth to mouth contact in this position, but she leaned down and blew on his lips. Almost a kiss. Better in some ways. Her breath was warm, like her, and he took her taste and scent into his mouth.

She kept moving. Her hips thrusting forward, taking him in and then out of her. Creating the friction with that deep slide into her. She moved faster, and faster, each deep move pulling him closer and closer.

She came first. Sabrina threw back her head. Her grip tightened on his chest. She clamped her teeth over her bottom lip, and her eyelids eased down. She made that sound again, deep within her throat.

Maybe it was that sound, or the tremors of her climax that did it for him. Maybe it was just because this was Sabrina. But Shaw didn't fight it.

He let her take him to the only place he wanted to go.

Chapter Thirteen

Don't think, Sabrina reminded herself.

Fortunately, her body was cooperating with that reminder. Sex with Shaw had left her buzzing and feeling, well, incredible. It was hard to think with all the pleasure still milling around inside her.

She took several moments, to settle her breathing and to allow herself time to drift back down to planet earth. It took even longer before she could look down at Shaw.

He was staring at her.

There was no lift in his eyebrow to indicate he was about to question what had just happened. His jaw muscles were relaxed, a rarity for him. But he didn't offer her a smile or romantic words.

He just continued to stare.

Maybe he was shell-shocked that he'd just had sex with her. Perhaps like her, his body was still numb with pleasure. Either way, the silence began to settle uncomfortably around them.

So did the awareness.

She was naked, except for the bra that Shaw had shoved down. Her breasts were exposed. *She* was exposed. And she suddenly felt the need to cover up.

Sabrina eased off of him, which took some effort. She was about as graceful as a drunk elephant, and there was no good side of her body that she wanted him to stare at. So, she got up from the sofa and began to gather her clothes.

"You're beautiful," Shaw said, sitting up and putting himself back into his shorts and jeans.

That stopped her. Sabrina glanced down at what she could see of her body and decided she obviously didn't see what he did.

"I'm eight months pregnant," she reminded him.

"And you're beautiful," he repeated. Shaw let the words linger between them for several seconds, and then he looked away and got up. "Get dressed. I'll order us some late breakfast."

She started to say something sexual, like she could have him for late breakfast, but Shaw's mind was obviously already on other things. He took out his phone and pressed in some numbers. He was indeed ordering food.

Since she didn't want to be standing around naked when it arrived, Sabrina gathered up her clothes and went into the bathroom so she could freshen up and dress. She didn't rush, hoping that the awkwardness she felt would fade by the time she went back into the main room.

It didn't.

Shaw was sitting on the sofa, his clothes all back in place, and he was talking on the phone. He glanced at her but kept it too brief for her to see what was really going on behind those stormy blue eyes.

Was he thinking about Fay?

No doubt. Sabrina certainly was. The sex had been easy. And incredibly satisfying. But it was clear that sex wasn't going to solve all their issues. It wasn't going to make them forget. Maybe though, just maybe, a sexual relationship could be the start of something else.

"What do you mean?" Shaw asked the caller. His tone was suddenly gruff and angry. "How did that happen?" He paused, and the tight jaw muscles returned. "Find him. And don't let him inside headquarters, understand?"

"What happened?" Sabrina asked the moment he ended the call.

"Newell slipped away from the officer who was tailing him."

"Just like Danny," she mumbled, and groaned.

"Not quite. Danny just got lucky when he got ahead of the tail, but Newell actually sneaked out of his apartment. He apparently went through the back window sometime, and the guard just realized what had happened."

Sneaking out the window didn't sound like something an innocent man would do. "You think he'll come here?"

"He might try, but the word will be out not to let him in."

That didn't mean he couldn't sneak into headquarters, or that he couldn't coax a friend to let him past watchful eyes.

"It'll be all right," Shaw said. It was something he was saying a lot lately. He tipped his head to her stomach. "How's the baby?"

"Quiet for a change. I hope she slept through all the noise of those loud gunshots."

"Yeah." That was all Shaw said. He reached to put his phone back into his pocket, but it buzzed before he could do that. His eyebrow did shoot up when he saw the name on his caller ID screen.

"It's Dr. Nicholson," he let her know, and he answered the call. "What can I do for you, Doctor?"

Sabrina couldn't hear what Dr. Nicholson was saying, but Shaw apparently didn't care much for it. "You can do that in just a minute, but first I'd like to know if you've heard from an old friend. Keith Newell." He paused. Listened. "So, you don't know where he is?"

Or else the doctor wasn't saying.

Still not looking pleased about this call, Shaw reached out to hand her the phone. "She wants to talk to you."

Sabrina's first thought was a bad one. The doctor had drawn her blood yesterday, and maybe something was wrong. She practically grabbed the phone from Shaw.

"Is this about the blood test?" Sabrina immediately asked.

"No. All your tests were fine. But I just found out from my business manager that the police are investigating me."

Until this call, Sabrina had forgotten that the investigation had extended to her OB.

Sabrina clicked on the speakerphone function of Shaw's phone. "They're not really investigating you." She stopped, looked at

Shaw, and he nodded for her to continue. "It's because of your friendship with a possible suspect."

"Officer Keith Newell," the doctor supplied. "Yes, as I just told the captain, Keith called me last night and said he's being railroaded, that Captain Tolbert is so anxious to make an arrest for the hostage crisis, that he's willing to ruin an innocent man's career."

"If Newell's innocent, that'll come out in the evidence." She hoped.

"Well, whatever comes out, I haven't done anything wrong. Keith and I are old friends. Nothing more." The doctor mumbled something that Sabrina couldn't understand, but she sounded frustrated. "If, and that's a big if, he's a dirty cop, he wouldn't have come to me." She paused. "What exactly do the police think I could have done to help him?"

"There's a DNA file and the DNA itself that was destroyed during the hostage standoff. It belonged to a newborn that's missing. His mother was murdered."

"And you think Keith did that?" the doctor snapped.

"He's just a possible suspect," Sabrina corrected. Then she paused. "Is he capable of that?"

"No."

"Even if it meant this dead woman could have hurt his career?" Sabrina pressed.

Dr. Nicholson wasn't so quick to answer this time. The seconds crawled by. "I don't think he would murder anyone." But she didn't sound convinced.

Neither was Sabrina.

"You should get another OB," Dr. Nicholson said. "You should be in the care of someone you trust completely. Obviously, I'm not that person."

Sabrina wanted to assure her that she did trust her. But it wasn't true.

The doubt was there.

"I'll contact some colleagues," the doctor continued. "I'll get some names of available OBs and call you back. I'll also send over some prenatal vitamins. With everything going on, I'm sure you haven't been taking them."

"I've missed a few days," Sabrina admitted. And she had no idea when she'd be able to go home and get them.

"Not to worry. I always have a supply here at the clinic, but I forgot to offer them to you yesterday. Should I send them to Captain Tolbert's office, since Keith said you'd been staying with the captain at the precinct?"

The question caused Sabrina to hesitate. It

didn't sound like a fishing-expedition type of question, but she wasn't exactly eager to volunteer her exact location. "Just phone the script into the pharmacy on St. Mary's, and I'll have someone pick it up for me."

Now, it was the doctor's turn to hesitate. "Of course. Good luck with this pregnancy, Sabrina. I wish you the best."

The doctor hung up, leaving Sabrina feeling frustrated and uncertain. Mercy. If the doctor was truly innocent, she was going to owe her a huge apology. But if Dr. Nicholson did have some part in this, even a small one, Sabrina didn't want to take any chances.

"I'm sorry," Shaw said.

Sabrina shrugged. "Couldn't be helped." Though she did hate the idea of having to find a new doctor this close to her delivery date.

"I'll call Lieutenant Rico in a few minutes and make arrangements for someone to pick up your prenatal vitamins," Shaw offered, just as there was a knock at the door. "Who is it?"

"Detective Luke Hennessey. I have your food and a report that Lieutenant Rico asked me to give you. I also have a message. The lieutenant said the report was important and that you'd want to read it right away."

Shaw stood and went to the door. He eased

it open and peered out at the young officer who was in the hall. He handed Shaw a brown delivery bag, the report and a large cup of coffee.

"Lieutenant Rico wanted you to know that Danny Monroe died during surgery."

Sabrina hadn't expected the news to hit her so hard, but it did. Part of her had hoped that Danny would pull through and be able to help them identify his boss. There was no chance of that happening now.

Shaw cursed, but then thanked the detective, and closed the door.

He immediately reset the lock.

It seemed absurd to take these kinds of security measures in police headquarters, but it had to be done.

"I didn't think Danny would make it," Shaw mumbled. But there was still disappointment that he hadn't.

Sabrina took out the food while Shaw read the report. There were several sandwiches, a fruit salad, two bottles of juice and one of milk, and she placed everything on the table. And waited. Whatever was in that report had captured Shaw's complete attention.

"At any point during the hostage standoff did one of the gunmen take your sandals?" he asked.

"No." But then she shook her head. "Wait a minute. When they were holding me at the office building, one of them, Burney, took them. He said it was so I wouldn't escape. There was broken glass on the floor, and he warned that it would cut my feet to shreds. But then, about ten minutes later, he brought the shoes back to me."

Shaw rubbed his fingers over his forehead and winced when he connected with one of the nicks. "Because evidence and trace just got around to examining them, and they found a tiny device that'd been affixed adjacent to the heel of your left shoe. It's a transmitter with eavesdropping capabilities. The heel was just high enough so that the receiver wouldn't hit the ground when you were walking."

Oh, mercy. So, the gunmen could have listened in on everything she and Shaw said from the moment he rescued her. "Did they put the device on me and then let me escape when you arrived at the abandoned building?"

"I don't think they *let* you do anything," Shaw said, staring at the report again. "I think this was their insurance policy. If you did manage to run, they would have been able to track you down."

Yes. And they'd tracked her down to the hotel room where they'd planned to take her hostage again. They'd probably also listened in to determine when the best time was to attack.

"So maybe Newell didn't leak our location," she suggested.

"Not necessarily. He could have followed the transmission to the hotel. Or he could have put it there after the fact so it would give us a reasonable doubt not to suspect him."

Yes. After all, they'd left Newell in the hotel room when she'd started cramping. Her bagged clothes and shoes had been there, and Newell would have had ample time to put a transmitter in place.

Shaw downed some of his coffee and motioned for her to eat, but he continued to read the report from Lieutenant Rico.

"The leak about the fake pacifier and the missing baby's DNA is making the rounds. Rico's already gotten some calls about it. A couple of reporters want to know if it was true, and it'll be the lead story on the noon news."

So, the word was out, and that meant the person responsible might be desperate to keep the information hidden. "What about the baby?"

Shaw shook his head. "He's still missing, but the FBI's involved now. They have a deep cover agent near the border, and he has connections to several black market baby brokers. He's been alerted in case the birth father is trying to sell the child."

Sabrina nearly choked on the sip of milk she'd just taken.

"It takes all kinds," Shaw mumbled.

There was a sound. Like a loud blast. And it brought Sabrina to her feet.

"A gunshot?" she asked Shaw.

He shook his head. "It was more like an explosion." Shaw took out his phone, but it buzzed before he could make a call. He checked the caller ID screen.

"It's Gavin," he relayed to her.

Sabrina groaned. She didn't want to go another round with Gavin, or any of the others. She wanted to know what had caused that sound. Mercy, they might have to evacuate. She only prayed this wasn't some other form of an attack.

Shaw put it on speaker. "How did you get this number?"

"From dispatch. I told them it was an emergency and I had to speak to you."

Shaw rolled his eyes. "What do you want?"

"You have to help me," Gavin said. It was clear from the man's tone that this wasn't one of his usual complaints. "Someone just tried to kill me."

Sabrina put her hand over her heart to steady it and moved closer to the phone.

"I'd parked my car in the lot across the street, and when I started toward it, the damn thing blew up." Gavin's voice got even louder. "Rouse is behind this. I know he is. I told you to arrest him."

"Where are you?" Shaw asked. Unlike Gavin, his voice was calm, but his expression wasn't.

"In the parking lot across from the headquarters building."

"You need to take cover in case the blast is just the beginning." Shaw hung up and made another call. "Lieutenant Rico, what's going on?"

"I'm not sure. It appears someone set a car bomb—"

There was a second blast, a loud crashing sound. Sabrina looked around, wondering if she should take cover.

What was happening?

"Lock down the place," Shaw ordered. "And get some men out there to see what's going on. I just got a call from Gavin Cunningham, and he said someone's trying to kill him."

But Sabrina wasn't sure Lieutenant Rico

heard the last part of Shaw's order because there was a third blast. Louder than the others.

This one shook the entire building.

And Sabrina got a whiff of something that caused her heart to pound even harder.

Smoke.

Chapter Fourteen

"What now?" Shaw cursed.

The building's fire alarm started, the shrill noise filling the flop room. The sound didn't do much to steady Shaw's nerves, which were already on full alert. His body was primed for a fight, but he hoped it wouldn't come down to that. There'd already been enough battles to last him a lifetime.

Shaw drew his gun and tried to finish the call with Lieutenant Rico. Whatever was going on out there, it couldn't be good, but maybe Rico already had everything under control. However, Shaw knew that wasn't the case when the lieutenant came back on the line.

"We have a big problem," Rico yelled over the piercing alarm. "In addition to the car bombs, someone set a fire in the men's bathroom. The fire department's on the way, and I have men responding with fire extinguishers.

But I'm short-staffed because a lot of officers are at the memorial service."

Well, that explained the smoke and the blasts. "How bad's the damage?"

"We're just now assessing the situation. But I can tell you the car bombs have broken windows and damaged other vehicles. We probably have some injuries. There were three blasts, two from the parking lot across the street and one from a car parked illegally curbside. We're closing off the area until the bomb squad can give us an all clear, but Captain, you should evacuate. We don't know if there are any other explosives or fires."

Hell, this was not what he wanted to hear.

"Keep me posted," Shaw ordered the lieutenant, and he put his phone away so his hands would be free.

There were no windows or secondary doors that he could use for evacuation, so he would have to get Sabrina out through the main hall. And he probably shouldn't delay. The smoke wouldn't be good for her or the baby, and that was especially true if the fire wasn't limited to the men's room.

"What's happening?" Sabrina asked.

He shook his head. "I'm not sure, but we have to get out of here now."

Her eyes widened, and her hands dropped

from her belly to her side. "Is it safe to do that?"

She looked terrified and likely was, but this was something he couldn't sugarcoat. "It should be safe, but just in case I want you to stay next to me, and if anything goes wrong, keep down."

Sabrina nodded. Then, she nodded again when he motioned for her to walk with him toward the door. She certainly didn't look confident about this, but then neither was Shaw. He couldn't wait though because if the fire spread, then they could be trapped in a burning building.

As if the building had heard him, the overhead sprinklers came on and began spraying water all over the room. And on them. Shaw tightened his grip on his weapon, disengaged the lock and cracked the door just a fraction so he could peer out into the hall.

He held his breath and braced himself for an attack.

Thankfully, there wasn't one. There were some officers scurrying toward the front of the building, but his end of the hall was empty.

Well, other than the spray from the sprinklers and a few wispy threads of smoke.

"Smoke," he mumbled under his breath. He remembered the fire at the hospital. The gunmen had used it as a literal smokescreen to help them escape.

Was this a smokescreen, too?

Was it meant to cover up something else that was going on?

If so, Shaw had to trust that his officers would put an end to it before it became a bigger threat. Right now, he had to focus all his energy on saving Sabrina.

"This way," he instructed her.

Sabrina moved directly behind him, but he could sense her hesitation when she realized the direction where they were headed. "We're going out through the dispatch exit?" she asked, her voice practically a shout over the fire alarms.

"Yeah." And Shaw was well aware that the last time he'd taken her through that door, Danny had fired shots at them. But Danny was dead, and he couldn't do a repeat attack. "The parking area off dispatch is secure. Guarded at all times. A person wouldn't have been able to get in there and plant a bomb."

He hoped. He also hoped another gunman wasn't perched on a rooftop.

Shaw continued to lead her down the hall, but he stopped when he reached an open office door to his left. No one appeared to be lurking there, ready to strike. But just in case, he checked that room and then over his shoulder.

Hell.

There were open doors behind them, too. At least a dozen of them. He hadn't considered open doors and empty rooms a threat before, but he certainly did now. He needed to hurry and get Sabrina out of there because he was getting a bad feeling about all of this.

"Why is this happening?" she asked.

Shaw heard her, but he didn't answer. He kept his attention on their surroundings. When they were outside and away from the blare of the alarms, he'd give her his theories. Maybe it was a terrorist attack. Or maybe it was an attack of the ordinary variety. If there was such a thing.

But he also had to consider that this was linked to everything that had been going on for the past two days. The hostages. Sabrina's kidnappings. The subsequent attacks. That's why he couldn't let down his guard. Nor could he hang around and take control of this new crime scene. He had to get Sabrina far away and to a safe house.

The tile floor was slick from the overhead sprinklers. Shaw slowed so Sabrina wouldn't slip. It seemed to take forever, but they finally made it to the door, and Shaw placed his hand on the push handle. He wouldn't just shove it wide open, though the smoke and the need to get Sabrina out of there made him want to do just that. But he couldn't. He had to make sure the area was indeed secure.

He didn't hear any sounds, other than the fire alarm, but Shaw felt the movement behind him. He turned, and in that split-second glimpse, he saw Sabrina.

Her eyes wide with fear. The gloved hand over her mouth.

And her attacker pressing a gun to her head.

SABRINA'S HEART SLAMMED against her chest.

Her breath froze.

She couldn't see the person who grabbed her from behind, but she felt his viselike grip on her shoulder. She felt it more when he hooked his arm around her neck and crushed her back against his chest.

In that same split second, he jammed the gun to her head.

She tried to call out to Shaw, but the person loosened his grip on her throat so he could slap his hand over her mouth. Not that Shaw would have heard her anyway over the noise.

But then Shaw looked back.

And no doubt saw that things had just gone from bad to worse.

Shaw automatically lifted his gun to aim it at her attacker, but the man's only response was to jam his own weapon even harder against her right temple. He didn't have to issue a verbal threat because Sabrina had no doubt that he would shoot her or Shaw.

The man shoved her forward to get her moving. Shaw moved, too. Without lowering his gun, he backed up until he ran into the door. Her attacker used the barrel of his weapon to motion for Shaw to open it.

Oh, God.

He was going to get them outside so he could kidnap her. But who was this, and why was he doing this to her again?

She tried to glance over her shoulder, but the man rammed his chest into her back and propelled her forward, almost into Shaw. The motion sent Shaw into the door again, and he must have hit the push handle, because it opened.

Sunlight spewed into the corridor, and she felt the fresh air reach her lungs. She still couldn't draw a full breath because her chest was tight with fear. She wasn't afraid for herself but for the baby and for Shaw.

Shaw continued to back up while he shot

volleying glances behind him, at her, and at her attacker. Could Shaw see the man's face? Did he know who was holding the gun on her?

Despite all the fear and the adrenaline, Sabrina tried to cut through the panic and figure out who was doing this. Rouse? Gavin? Maybe even Newell? It certainly wasn't Dr. Nicholson, but then maybe it was no one she even knew.

This could be yet another hired gun.

At the gunman's urging, Sabrina stepped from the building. So did he, and he kicked the door shut behind them. He also maneuvered her so that she was turned toward the dispatch officer, who drew his weapon the moment he spotted them. The gunman was using her as a human shield.

What should she do?

The adrenaline was knifing through her now, and it was hard to keep control of her breathing. Much more of this, and she'd hyperventilate. The only thing that kept her from totally losing it was Shaw. Even though his gaze was fastened on the gunman, Shaw was right there, and she believed with all her heart he would do whatever it took to get her out of this.

But she needed to help.

How?

She glanced around, looking for a weapon or something she could possibly grab if she got the chance.

There wasn't anything.

Sabrina considered dropping to the ground. Yes, the fall would be risky, but it wasn't as risky as having that gun pointed at her head. Even if the man's immediate plan wasn't to shoot her, something could still go wrong.

The dispatch officer reached for something on the desk just below the keys. A phone. But the gunman obviously saw what was happening.

He turned his gun and fired.

Sabrina braced herself for the gunshot blast, but it was merely a swooshing sound, barely audible over the noise of the fire alarms. That's when she realized he was using a gun rigged with a silencer.

The dispatch officer collapsed onto the ground, and his gun fell from his hand, landing on the concrete next to him. She wasn't sure if he was dead, but he certainly wasn't moving, and there was blood.

Too much.

The gunman positioned her again, moving her closer to the man he'd just shot, and he kicked the gun out of reach. He didn't waste any time, and he shoved her forward again. He pulled a set of keys and some kind of remote control from the hooks above the table, and he pressed the button on the keypad so the car's security system made a loud beep. The lights flashed, and in doing so it identified which car went with the keys he'd taken.

He pushed her in that direction.

Her stomach clenched. He was planning to put her in that car and make a getaway, and unless something happened soon in their favor, Shaw wasn't going to have a clear shot to stop this monster.

She stared at Shaw, hoping he'd be able to convey to her what she should do. But he only focused on the gunman while they made their way to the car.

When they reached the vehicle, the gunman motioned for Shaw to drop his weapon. "Now!" he growled when Shaw didn't comply. He moved his gun from her temple to her stomach.

To the baby.

The fear slammed through her. The threat had been horrible enough when it'd been directed at her, but this SOB was threatening to hurt her baby.

Sabrina tried to figure out who'd spoken that threat and launched them into this nightmare, but it was obvious he was trying to disguise his voice. Still, Shaw could no doubt see his face, and unless he was wearing a mask, Shaw knew who they were up against.

Shaw dropped his gun.

Her heart dropped with it.

He was surrendering. He was giving up!

Part of her wanted to scream, to beg him to pick up his gun again, but she knew she had no choice. He couldn't risk the baby being hurt.

The gunman kicked Shaw's weapon under the car, and he took the barrel from her stomach and put it back to her temple. Of course, both she and the baby would die if he shot her point-blank, but she preferred that he keep the gun on her.

But he didn't.

The gunman aimed it at Shaw.

"Inside the car," he ordered, his voice still low and raspy.

This wasn't any better. True, the baby was temporarily safe, but now he had a clean shot of Shaw.

The man kept a tight grip on her, moving his hand from her mouth back to her throat. He squeezed hard and used that pressure to get her moving. He opened the back door of the unmarked car and backed in first so that he was seated. He hauled her next to him, keeping her positioned so that she still couldn't see his face.

Sabrina considered elbowing him in the gut. She was in the perfect position to do just that. But he had that gun pointed right at Shaw. If she did anything, he would fire.

"Shut the door and drive," he ordered Shaw. He tossed the keys onto the front seat.

Shaw stood there a moment, and she could see the argument he was having with himself. She was having the same argument. But it was cut short when the gunman scraped the silencer across her cheek. The pain was instant with the metal digging into her skin. He no doubt drew blood. Sabrina didn't yell out in pain, but it sickened her that this person had total control over her, her baby and Shaw.

The veins popped out on Shaw's neck and forehead, and his hands clenched into fists. For a moment, Sabrina thought he might risk everything and launch himself at the gunman.

He didn't.

When the gunman started to make another cut on her cheek, Shaw cursed and hurried around the front of the car. He glanced at the fallen dispatch officer and no doubt wanted to call for help. He didn't do that, either. Shaw threw open the car door, got behind the wheel and started the engine.

"Where to?" Shaw asked.

He met her gaze in the rearview mirror, and Sabrina tried her best to look brave and in control. Shaw had enough on his plate without worrying whether or not she would panic and make this situation even more dangerous than it already was.

"Just drive," the gunman snarled.

Shaw did. He put the car in gear and drove. He didn't get far before she saw the security gate. It was tall and metal, and she thought it might stop them. But the gunmen pushed the button on the remote control he'd taken with the keys. The gate slid open.

And Shaw drove through.

"Go left," the gunman instructed.

A left turn would take them away from the front of the headquarters building and away from the chaos that was going on there because of the car bombings. There were so many officers in the area, all of them scrambling amid the smoke and the fires that the bombs had created. She saw several injured people lying on the street and sidewalks.

But no one seemed to notice them.

Probably because of the heavily tinted windows on the vehicle. Or maybe because they thought she and Shaw were merely evacuating the area as Lieutenant Rico has advised them to do. No one was running to help.

She and Shaw were on their own.

Sabrina turned slightly so she could keep watch behind them, hoping that the car would get someone's attention.

And that's when she saw her attacker's sleeve.

She immediately recognized the shade of blue. And her heart sank even further.

The gunman was a cop.

Chapter Fifteen

Shaw considered a couple of options. None ideal. One was to slam on his brakes and hope the sudden stop would allow him to wrestle the gun away from their would-be kidnapper.

But the guy could still get off a shot.

A shot that could hurt Sabrina.

A second option was to hit another car, preferably a parked one. Or he could run a red light. Anything that would get the attention of his officers. But those weren't risk free, either. Sabrina wasn't wearing a seat belt, and God knew where or how she might land if there was even a light collision.

He couldn't risk it.

And that left only one other option. Somehow, he had to reach over the back of the seat and just grab that gun away from the cop SOB who had it pointed right at Sabrina.

One of his own was responsible for this. Officer Newell was the likely candidate.

Well, maybe.

The guy was wearing a uniform, but Shaw couldn't see his face because it was covered with a latex superhero mask. A fake face and maybe a fake uniform.

Or possibly a stolen one.

How the hell had this guy gotten all the way down the hall of police headquarters dressed like that?

He probably hadn't put on the mask until he was out of sight from the other officers and until he'd gotten close enough to the flop room. And with that uniform, he had likely walked right past everyone. With all the commotion going on from the car bombings and the bathroom fire, no one would have noticed an officer in a hurry. Obviously no one had seen him and gotten suspicious.

"Where are we going?" Shaw asked.

He adjusted the rearview mirror so he could get a better look at Sabrina. Other than that scratch on her face, she seemed okay. *Seemed.* She had to be scared out of her mind. And Shaw would make this armed bastard pay for that scratch and for her fear.

"Just drive," the guy growled.

Their captor was trying to disguise his

voice, and it was working. Shaw couldn't tell who the heck this was, and it didn't help that their three major suspects were all about the same height and weight.

"Go right," the guy suddenly barked.

Again, Shaw looked for some escape route or some diversion he could use, but unfortunately people were starting to head out for lunch breaks, and the sidewalks were filled with pedestrians. There were also plenty of cars on the street.

Shaw took the right turn a little faster than he normally would have, the tires squealing in protest at the excessive speed, and he watched the gunman shift in the backseat. The mask slipped a little, only enough to see the guy's neck. It certainly didn't provide Shaw with an ID.

Right now, his best hope was that someone had found the wounded dispatch officer and had notified Rico that an unmarked car was missing. If that happened, the car could be tracked since it was equipped with GPS.

But that was a big if.

There was a lot going on at headquarters, and they were short on officers. It might take an hour or more for anyone to figure out what was going on. By then, they could be into the next county.

Or dead.

But Shaw rethought that.

If the gunman had wanted them dead, he would have just shot them in the hall at the headquarters. He wouldn't have orchestrated a very risky kidnapping.

So, this went back to motive.

Someone intended to use Sabrina for leverage to get him to do something illegal. Probably something to do with that missing baby and the DNA that had been destroyed during the hostage standoff.

Of course, it could be something else.

Shaw thought of the false info that the police had leaked about the missing baby's DNA from a pacifier. The leak had also revealed that the police would soon have the DNA extracted from it.

This guy probably thought the leak was real, and if so, he would want Shaw to destroy the so-called evidence. Shaw considered trying to tell him the truth, that there was no pacifier, but the gunman likely wouldn't believe him, and even if he did, then what?

At best, the gunman might just let them go because they hadn't seen his face. But if that happened, it would mean not finding the location of the baby. Maybe it was because Shaw was so close to becoming a father that he knew that couldn't happen. The baby had to be found, but the trick was to do that without endangering Sabrina and his own child.

"Let Sabrina go," Shaw tried. "I'm the one who can help you with whatever this is all about. She'll just be in the way."

The gunman made a *yeah-right* sound that didn't need clarification. Without Sabrina, the guy had nothing to make Shaw cooperate. She and the unborn child were the ultimate bargaining tools, and this bozo knew that.

"Go left," the guy ordered.

Shaw did, and he immediately recognized the area. There was no traffic on this particular side street because most of the buildings were old and abandoned. Including the one at the end of the street. The one still roped off with ragged yellow crime scene tape.

It was the building where the gunmen had taken Sabrina after the hostage situation.

"Stop by the silver car," the gunman added.

There was indeed a silver Ford parked at the side entrance, and Shaw pulled up next to it. He looked inside the vehicle, praying this guy didn't have reinforcements, but the vehicle appeared to be empty.

The guy shoved open the door, and with the gun still pointed at her head, he dragged

Sabrina out. Again, he put her right in front of him and led her in the direction of the silver car. Shaw walked in that direction, as well.

"No!" the gunman ordered Shaw. "Get on your knees, hands behind your head."

That put a knot in Shaw's stomach, but he didn't jump to any conclusions just yet. However, the conclusions came anyway when the man opened the car and pushed Sabrina onto the front passenger seat.

"On your knees!" the gunman repeated to Shaw.

Maybe he'd been wrong about the guy's motive. Maybe he didn't want Shaw to do anything illegal after all. Because it was possible the gunman intended to shoot him execution style, right in front of Sabrina. And that left Shaw with a question even more troubling than his possible murder.

What would happen to Sabrina and their baby if he was killed?

With this sick SOB behind the trigger, Shaw didn't like any of the answers that came to mind.

And that's why he had to do something now, before the gunman managed to get away with her.

Shaw put his hands behind his head. Slowly.

While he calculated the distance between him and the gunman.

About ten feet.

Sabrina was in the car, certainly not out of the line of fire, but at least she wasn't standing out in the open. However, she did have a gun pointed at her head, and the guy's finger was definitely positioned on the trigger.

Shaw would have one chance to save her.

Just one.

Shaw took a deep breath and started to lower himself as if he were dropping to his knees. But he didn't.

"Get down!" Shaw shouted to Sabrina.

He couldn't risk waiting to see if she could manage to do that. There was no time. It was now or maybe never.

Shaw lowered his head and charged the gunman.

SABRINA HEARD SHAW SHOUT for her to get down, but it took a split second for that to register. In that split second, she saw Shaw run head first toward the gunman.

The gunman fired.

And Sabrina screamed.

It couldn't end this way. She couldn't lose Shaw now, not after everything they'd managed to survive.

Shaw rammed his body into the gunman, and they landed against the car door. It slammed shut, and because she was already precariously perched on the seat, the momentum threw her off balance and her hip rammed into the gear shift.

She quickly tried to right herself so she could help, but the two were in a fierce battle for the gun. Shaw had clamped on to the gunman's right wrist and had both his hand and gun smashed against the window.

Frantically, she looked for any sign of blood or injury, but she couldn't tell if Shaw had been shot. And she wasn't sure about the best way to help him.

She searched the car, shoving aside newspapers and a fast-food bag. No cell phone. No gun. Nothing she could use as a weapon. But she couldn't just sit there, either, with Shaw in a fight for their lives.

Sabrina crawled over the gear shift and into the driver's seat. No keys. But there was a horn, and she jammed her hand against it. The sound blared, and she didn't let up. Maybe someone would hear the noise and call the police. Of course, this wasn't the best area of the city so it was possible something like a car horn would be ignored.

There was a hard thump against the

passenger-side window, and her breath froze. Because it sounded like another shot. She tried to pick through the tangle of the two bodies so she could determine what was happening.

The men were still locked in a fierce battle, and the weapon was still pointed upward, thanks to Shaw's unrelenting grip. But the gunman was using his left fist to pound Shaw in his midsection. With each blow, the gunman's elbow rammed into the glass. Neither was giving up.

But she wouldn't, either.

"Run, Sabrina!" Shaw yelled. He wanted her to try to get away, but she didn't want to leave him like this.

Still, she could try to go for help, especially since the horn didn't seem to be drawing anyone's attention. She threw open the door and climbed out.

Just as there was another shot.

She ducked down, putting her hands over her belly to protect the baby.

The shot went through the passenger window and into the front windshield, shattering both. If she'd stayed put inside the car, she would have almost certainly been hit.

That both terrified her and infuriated her.

She didn't care what their kidnapper's motives were, but she was sick and tired of his total disregard for Shaw's life and the life she carried inside her.

The anger shot through her, and Sabrina looked around. Not for an escape route. But for a rock or a fallen tree limb, anything she could use to hit the guy.

Sabrina quickly spotted several small stones. They weren't much bigger than silver dollars, but she gathered them up, drew back her hand and threw them with as much force as she could. They smacked the gunman in the back of the neck.

It wasn't much of a blow, but it caused him to react by jerking his head to the side. Shaw took full advantage of that slight maneuver and bashed the gunman's hand against the metal rim of the door.

The gun went flying.

And Sabrina didn't waste any time running after it.

She made her way around the front of the car, all the while looking on the ground to see where the weapon had landed. She finally spotted it next to the unmarked car the gunman had used to kidnap them.

She raced toward it.

But didn't get far.

The gunman made a loud, feral-sounding

growl. And he shoved Shaw backward—right toward her.

Sabrina barely got out of the way in time.

Shaw fell to the ground, his back just a few inches from the weapon. Sabrina tried to tell him that, but she didn't get the chance. The gunman dove at Shaw and landed on him with his full weight.

Sabrina heard Shaw gasp for breath, and she prayed he wasn't injured. She still couldn't see if he'd been shot, but he did have blood on his face, possibly from a blow the gunman had managed to land.

She reached for the gun again, but the men shifted, rolling toward her, and trapping the gun beneath them.

The fight continued with the sounds of muscle and bone slamming against muscle and bone. Drops of blood and sweat spewed in every direction, some of them landing on her.

Sabrina maneuvered herself around them, hoping she'd have an opportunity to get that gun. Once she had it, she and Shaw could gain control of the situation.

Well, maybe.

And maybe the guy would force her to shoot him. She would. She would do whatever it took to get Shaw and their baby out of this alive.

The men rolled around, jockeying for position, and the fight continued, each of them slamming their fists into the other.

Finally, she saw the gun and reached for it. But the gunman must have seen what she was trying to do, because he threw out his fist, slamming it into her leg.

The pain shot through her, and she gave a loud groan, but she didn't give up.

Neither did Shaw.

That punch the gunman had delivered to her leg seemed to give Shaw a new burst of adrenaline. The muscles in his face turned to iron, and he drew back his fist and slammed it, hard, into the gunman's jaw.

Shaw didn't stop there. He drew back his hand and delivered another punch. And another. Until the gunman dropped his head back on the ground. He appeared to be unconscious. But maybe he was just pretending to be so that they'd let down their guard.

Sabrina wasn't letting anything down. She grabbed the gun and tossed it to Shaw. His hands were cut and bleeding, but he snatched it in midair and jammed it right against the gunman's throat.

"Move and you die," Shaw growled, though

she had no idea how he spoke with his teeth clenched that tightly. "Personally, I hope you choose to move."

The threat was clear and real, and the gunman must have realized that because his hands dropped limply to his sides.

Shaw used his left hand to take out his cell phone, and he passed it to Sabrina. "Call for backup," he instructed.

Her hand was shaking, but she took the phone and pressed in nine-one-one.

"What's your emergency?" the dispatcher immediately answered.

Sabrina fought with her ragged breath so she could answer, so she could give the dispatcher enough information to get backup on the way.

She watched as Shaw reached for the guy's latex mask, and he pulled it off with a fierce jerk.

And Sabrina finally saw the gunman's face.

Chapter Sixteen

Shaw stared down into the gunman's eyes, and he prayed the guy would move so he'd have an excuse to beat him senseless.

Or worse.

He had to rein in his anger because it was obvious that merely catching the gunman wasn't going to solve this investigation.

Gavin Cunningham stared back at him, not with fear in his eyes. Definitely no remorse, either. But there was some defiance, and despite Gavin's bruised and bloody face, he managed a dry smile.

"Backup's on the way," Sabrina relayed to him.

While he kept the gun point-blank on Gavin, Shaw glanced at her. Despite everything that had just happened, she looked amazingly well. She certainly wasn't cowering in fear, but like him, she was glaring at Gavin. She had a right to glare. Gavin had manhandled her, kidnapped her and would have done God knows what else if he'd managed to escape with her.

Later, Shaw would hold her and tell her how thankful he was that she and the baby were okay. But for now, there was something more pressing.

The missing baby.

Shaw moved back a little, to put an arm's length between Gavin and him, and he got to work. "I'm guessing you did all this to cover up the fact that you murdered a young woman and stole the child that you'd conceived with her. I figure you hired Burney and his brother to steal the DNA file. You also hired one or both to kill her. They did, but then a lot of things started to go wrong."

Gavin shook his head. "I'm not confessing to anything."

"You don't have to. The DNA from the baby's pacifier will tell us everything we need to know," he lied. Because there was no DNA from the baby to compare to Gavin's. Still, Gavin didn't know that. "So, here's the deal, tell me where you hid your son, and I'll tell the DA you cooperated."

"Right." Gavin's tone was cocky, and Shaw had to fight his rage again.

He really wanted to pound this moron to dust.

"Right," Shaw repeated, trying to put all that rage inside him into a calm, smug veneer. He was a veteran cop, and he had to shove the personal stuff aside so he could get this bastard.

"I guess you don't mind getting the death penalty," Shaw commented. Now, he smiled. "Ever watched someone get a needle shoved in their arm? Contrary to popular belief, it isn't painless. It's a slow agonizing death."

Gavin just stared at him.

"Tell me where the baby is," Shaw demanded.

Gavin chuckled. "No way. A trial could last for years. And a lot could happen to a baby in all that time."

Sabrina made a sound of outrage. "Give me the gun," she demanded. "You're a cop and you're bound by the badge not to shoot him, but I will."

She would, too. Shaw could tell from that steely look that she wasn't bluffing.

Gavin volleyed glances between her and Shaw, and by degrees his smile faded. It faded even more when there was the sound of sirens approaching. It wouldn't be long, mere minutes, before backup arrived.

"Get up," Shaw ordered the man.

Gavin's eyes widened. "Why?"

"Because you're resisting arrest, that's why." Shaw lifted the gun gripped in his hand. "And I'm going to shoot you for resisting."

"You wouldn't do that," Gavin spat out.

"Yes. I. Would." And Shaw left no doubt that he was telling the truth. And it was the truth. It would cost him his badge, but by God he was going to find that missing baby before it was too late. "Get up!"

Gavin struggled to get to his feet. His eyes were wild and wide now, and he looked around as he expected someone to come to his aid.

Shaw aimed the gun at Gavin's left shoulder. "Last chance, where's the baby?"

Gavin lifted his hands, palm out. "You'll shoot an unarmed man?"

"In a heartbeat." Shaw tightened his finger on the trigger and got ready to fire.

"Stop!" Gavin yelled. "You're crazy, you know that?"

Shaw fired a shot over Gavin's shoulder and lowered the gun so the next bullet would hit the intended target. "Where's the baby?" Shaw didn't change his tone or his body language, because he was already sending the message he wanted to send.

"Okay," Gavin mumbled. And there was no cockiness in that. "Take the death penalty off the table, and I'll tell you where the kid is."

Shaw thought about it a second. "I'll take the death penalty off the table."

Gavin nodded, blew out several short breaths. "The baby's at one-one-two St. Martin's Street, just two blocks from here. He's safe. He wasn't hurt when Burney and Danny took him from his mother. Right now, he's with a nanny I hired. Her name is Peggy Watford."

Shaw heard the backup officers take the turn onto the street. He kept the gun aimed at Gavin. "Give me your phone." And Shaw knew he had one because it was clipped to the man's belt. Gavin removed it, gave it to Shaw, and he passed it to Sabrina.

"What's the phone number of the place where the nanny has the baby?" Shaw demanded. "Sabrina's going to call and make sure you aren't lying. If you are, one bullet will go in your shoulder. The other in your leg. I haven't decided yet where the third bullet will go."

Gavin's voice was a tangle of nerves when he rattled off the number. Sabrina quickly dialed it, just as the cruiser with the backup officers came to a stop.

"Don't tell her who you are," Shaw instructed Sabrina. "Once you hear her voice, hang up."

Sabrina nodded and put the call on speaker.

It seemed to take forever for the call to connect. Shaw waited, knowing he wasn't leaving this scene until he had confirmed the whereabouts of the child.

"Get officers to one-one-two St. Martin's Street," Shaw ordered his backup, just in case. "I want confirmation ASAP that a newborn baby is there. Call me as soon as you know something."

"Mr. Cunningham," a woman finally answered. She'd obviously seen Gavin's number on her caller ID. "I didn't expect you to phone until later. The baby's fine, though. He's sleeping. And I'll have him ready tonight for the trip, just like you wanted."

Shaw motioned for Sabrina to click off the phone, and she did.

"I told you the kid was all right," Gavin insisted. "I wouldn't hurt a baby, even if his mother was nothing but trash."

Shaw didn't believe that because, after all, Gavin hadn't cared a lick about Sabrina's baby.

"What do you plan to do with him?" Sabrina asked.

The backup officers moved in, and Shaw motioned for them to cuff Gavin. One of the cops also read the man his rights. However, that didn't stop Gavin from answering Sabrina's question.

"A friend of a friend has an adoption agency. I'd made arrangements for the kid to be picked up tonight. He was going to a good family."

Maybe. Or maybe Gavin planned to sell the child. "Why did you think you'd get away with it?"

Gavin lifted his shoulder as the cuffs snapped shut, locking his hands behind him. Apparently, Gavin didn't intend to add anything to his meager confession.

But Shaw figured he knew the rest. "My guess is you were trying to set up Wilson Rouse, to make it look as if he's the one who killed the woman and took the child." Too bad Gavin's sick plan had come close to succeeding. "Rouse probably isn't even your biological father."

The corner of Gavin's mouth lifted. "But he is. That's the kicker. He really is my dear dad, thanks to a roll between the sheets with the hired help thirty years ago."

Oh, yeah. Then the plan would have indeed worked.

Gavin could have claimed that Rouse not only wanted to get rid of his illegitimate son but his less than worthy grandson, as well. Rouse would have fought the charges, might have even won, but his name and reputation would have been ruined. And Gavin would have been long gone or the evidence destroyed so that no one could ever connect him to the dead woman.

"I won't spend my life in prison," Gavin insisted. Some of the cockiness had returned. "I'm a good lawyer, and I have people on my side."

"Don't be so sure of that," Shaw countered. "Your uptown law partners won't like the scandal, either. I'm betting they dump you hard and fast."

Shaw walked to Sabrina, slipped his arm around her waist and pulled her to him. He looked down at her, deep into her eyes. "Are you okay?"

She nodded. "You?"

He tried to keep things light. "I'm too old to get in fistfights."

But his attempt failed because the tears sprang to her eyes. "You could have been killed." Her voice broke, and she buried her face against his shoulder.

"How touching," Gavin called out, and the officers led him to the cruiser. "You can come and visit me in jail while I'm appealing my life sentence."

Shaw glanced at the man. "I took the death penalty off the table, but the DA didn't. It's his call, and I'm betting with the murders at the hospitals and the havoc you've caused, the death penalty is guaranteed. I know I'll do everything to make sure that happens."

Gavin looked as if the breath had been knocked out of him.

Good.

It was a small matter of satisfaction, but Shaw knew it wouldn't stop the nightmares. He might never be able to forget what Gavin had put Sabrina through.

"I'm in love with you," he heard Sabrina say.

He was so deep in his thoughts that it took Shaw a moment to realize what she said.

"It's true," she added before he could speak. "I realized it when Gavin fired the shot, and I didn't know if it'd hit you or not." She sniffed, wiped away tears. "I knew then that I'm in love with you. And it doesn't have anything to do with carrying your child. Or the great sex. That only makes me love you more, but it's not the reason I'm in love with you."

She opened her mouth, probably to continue to convince him that what she felt was the real thing. But Shaw didn't need to be convinced. He could see the love in her eyes.

So, he kissed her.

There were bits of grass and dirt on his mouth, and he pulled back to wipe it off, but Sabrina grabbed a fistful of his shirt and yanked him back to her to continue the kiss anyway. She didn't stop until she had to breathe, and when she broke the kiss, she gasped for air.

"I'm in love with you because…" She stopped, blinked back more tears. "Because you're you."

Shaw was sure he blinked, too. It was a simple reason. The best of reasons.

Now, it was his turn to kiss her.

"Sir?" one of the officers called out. "You want us to wait until a unit arrives to pick up you and Ms. Carr to take you to headquarters?"

Sabrina looked at him, then at the officer who'd asked the question. "Is it safe to go back to headquarters?" Shaw wanted to know.

"Yes. The fire's out. It was more smoke than anything."

Smoke. No doubt to create the diversion. A diversion that had worked.

Well, temporarily.

"Don't wait," Shaw instructed. "Get Mr. Cunningham to the jail for processing. And have someone call me the second you have news about the missing baby."

"Yes, sir," the officer assured him. He got into the cruiser where Gavin was locked into the backseat, and he drove away.

Shaw doubted it would be long before their ride arrived, so he decided to make this quick. Once they did return to headquarters, he'd be swamped with the tail end of this investigation.

First though, he wanted to clear up some things with Sabrina.

"It's okay," she continued while he was trying to gather his thoughts. "You don't have to say or do anything. I just wanted you to know."

He kissed her again, hoping to use the time to find the right words. It was a bad decision. The kiss turned hot and deep, and it clouded his mind even more.

Finally, Shaw just put an end to the kissing and caught her shoulders. "I'm in love with you, too, Sabrina."

She stood there. Staring. And she looked as

stunned as Gavin had when the officers had hauled him away.

"You're in love with me?" she challenged.

"Yeah. And the only reason I have is the same as yours. Because you're you. Because you're a good, decent, kind, caring woman who'd do anything in the world for me, including giving me this precious child."

He slid his hand over her belly.

Her tears started again, and she launched herself at him. Shaw pulled her as close as the baby would allow, and he kissed her again. This time, he kept it short so it wouldn't numb his mind, and he geared up to finish what he'd started.

"Fay—" he said.

But Sabrina pressed her fingers to his mouth. "You don't have to tell me. I know you'll always love Fay. I don't expect you to feel the same way about me as you did about her."

Surprised, he blinked. "Well, you should. Because I love you as much as I loved her when she was alive. But she's not alive anymore, and we are. We're both here, in love with each other, and I can't help but believe that's exactly what Fay would have wanted."

Sabrina stopped, drew in her breath, and

she finally nodded. "It is what she would have wanted. She loved us both."

"And we both loved her," Shaw finished. "But Sabrina, you don't deserve anything less than my whole heart, and that's what I'm offering you."

"Ohhhh." She moved her hand to her own mouth to press back a sob. Thankfully, it sounded like a happy sob. "But how can you truly forgive me for Fay's death?"

She had mentally skirted around this for days, but he already knew the answer. "Easy. I blamed you. Myself. But I was wrong. Neither of us is responsible for what happened." He leaned in and kissed her. "Fay is the one who brought us together. She's the one who wanted us to raise this baby, and I'll always be thankful to her for that, for giving me you."

Sabrina's breath trembled from her tears, and she reached out to him.

But then, his phone buzzed.

He glanced down at the caller ID and saw that it was Lieutenant Rico. Shaw cursed and answered it.

"We have the baby, and he's okay," Rico said, obviously not bothering with a greeting. Shaw didn't want one. That was the best news he could have gotten.

"Thanks. I'll be back in a few minutes."

Shaw hung up and hoped those few minutes were enough. "The baby's safe," he relayed to Sabrina.

The relief flooded through her, and he could feel it in every part of her body when she hugged him. Shaw was just as relieved as she was, but he cut the celebration short.

"I want to get married," he blurted out, and winced at his abrupt tone. Sheez. He'd negotiated hostage standoffs that hadn't given him this much trouble.

"Let me try that again," Shaw corrected. "Will you marry me?"

He braced himself for another of her shocked looks, maybe even some hesitation, but her hug got harder, and she found his mouth with hers.

"Yes," she said, a split second before she kissed him.

Yes.

That part registered in Shaw's brain, but the kiss even managed to fog that up a little.

"That was a yes?" he questioned, pulling back just a little.

He kept his mouth right over hers so he could take in her taste with each breath. It was a taste he knew he would want for the rest of his life.

"A definite yes." But now, she hesitated. "I have a condition, though."

He thought maybe his heart stopped. She couldn't back out. He wouldn't let her. Sabrina was his.

"What?" he asked cautiously. He was willing to agree to anything.

"Marry me before the baby comes. I want us to be a real family."

He hadn't realized he'd been holding his breath until it swooshed out of him. "Deal. The wedding before the baby. But the last condition isn't really a condition."

"Why?"

He shrugged. That was the easiest question he'd ever had to answer. "Because we're already a family."

And to prove it, Shaw kissed her so that neither of them would ever forget it.

Chapter Seventeen

Two Weeks Later

Sabrina clamped her teeth over her bottom lip to stop herself from screaming. She'd read all the books about the pain management. She'd prepared herself.

Or so she'd thought.

But nothing could have prepared her for this.

"It's okay," Shaw told her. But his strained voice and expression didn't exactly convey that all was okay.

He looked scared spitless.

Sabrina wasn't scared. She was in too much pain to feel anything but the contractions that had hold of her stomach. Mercy. It was relentless.

"Push," Dr. Nicholson instructed.

The delivery bed was angled high enough so that Sabrina could see the doctor, but Dr.

Nicholson had her attention focused on the birth.

Sabrina pushed, and dug her shoes into the stirrups so she could bear down. The ivory peep-toe heels looked absurd against the metal stirrups. For that matter, she probably looked absurd since she was still wearing her lacy cream-colored wedding dress.

Shaw still had on his tux, even though the tie was off and God knew where. It'd been a crazy, frantic ride from the church to the hospital. Things hadn't settled down after their arrival, either. Once Dr. Nicholson checked Sabrina, she had her rushed to the delivery room.

There'd been no time for prep. No time to change into a hospital gown.

No time for anything but the pain.

"Okay, stop pushing," the doctor told her. "We need to wait for the next contraction, but it won't be long."

No doubt. The contractions were only seconds apart, and Sabrina barely had time to catch her breath in between them.

"I'm sorry," Shaw said, shaking his head.

He was right next to her, gripping her left hand. A position he'd taken the instant they'd been ushered into the delivery room.

"Sorry for what?" Sabrina asked while she fought with her breath.

"I didn't know you'd hurt this much." Well, he certainly wasn't the calm, collected police captain now. His nerves were right there on the surface. "I'm so sorry. I wish I could do something. Anything."

"You've done enough," she joked.

Even though Sabrina had no idea how she managed to attempt humor. This didn't feel funny.

She had to bite her lip again to stop herself from yelling. Or cursing. Sheez, how did women go through this multiple times?

"Push," the doctor ordered.

Unlike Shaw, Dr. Nicholson sounded totally in control. And looked it, too. It made Sabrina glad that they had mended fences after Gavin's arrest. She wouldn't have wanted another doctor for this because Dr. Nicholson had been there with her from the beginning.

Thankfully, Shaw had mended his own fences with Officer Newell, and everything was back to normal at headquarters.

Sabrina pressed her peep-toes against the stirrups again and pushed as hard as she could. The pain was blinding, and she used every bit of her energy to fight to maintain the push that the doctor had ordered.

"You're doing great, Sabrina," Dr. Nicholson told her. "Keep it up."

Sabrina cursed in spite of her attempts not to. She wasn't doing great. She was hurting!

But just like that, the pain stopped. Something inside her seemed to give way. The pressure was gone. The contraction ended.

And then Sabrina heard the cry.

It was a sound that touched every part of her body, and she looked in stunned amazement as Dr. Nicholson lifted the baby so she could see.

"It's a boy," the doctor announced.

A boy.

She and Shaw had a son.

"Well, despite being two weeks early, he has healthy lungs," Dr. Nicholson added over the baby's loud cries. "Have you guys picked out a name?"

She and Shaw had chosen the names Elizabeth Sabrina Tolbert for a girl or Jacob Shaw Tolbert for a boy.

So, this was Jacob.

But Sabrina couldn't speak. She looked at Shaw, who seemed as dumbfounded as she was.

"Okay, you can tell me the name later. Captain Dad, it's time to cut the umbilical cord." Dr. Nicholson put the baby on Sabrina's stomach and handed Shaw the scissors.

Shaw took the scissors. Sabrina saw that part, but then she zoomed in on that tiny precious crying face. It was wrinkled and red, but it was the most beautiful face she'd ever seen.

Jacob Shaw Tolbert had his daddy's dark hair. Shaw's chin and mouth, too. But Sabrina could see the shape of her own eyes in him.

The love was instant. Powerful. Unconditional. And it became complete when the doctor wrapped Jacob in a blanket and put him in her arms.

"Are you still in pain?" Shaw asked. He kissed her cheek. Her forehead. And then he kissed the baby. The nervous flurry of kisses continued.

Sabrina definitely wasn't hurting. In fact, had there been pain? She was no longer sure. Her body was humming now, and she felt higher than the moon and stars.

She smiled. "No pain," she assured him.

Because Shaw still looked terrified, she leaned over and kissed him on the mouth.

He kissed her right back.

"I need to borrow this little guy for a second so I can weigh him," the attending nurse said.

She took the baby and placed him on a table not too far from the delivery bed.

The doctor finished up with Sabrina and pulled off her gloves. "You did great. All three of you. I'll arrange to have you taken to a private room, but from the looks of things, you won't have to stay more than a day."

"Thank you," Sabrina and Shaw said in unison.

"For everything," Sabrina added.

The doctor smiled, nodded, and Sabrina saw her blink away some happy tears.

"He's six pounds, fourteen ounces," the nurse relayed. "Twenty-one inches long. And he just peed on me." The nurse laughed.

So did Shaw and Sabrina.

Every little detail was amazing. So were his cries. And the little foot kicks. The hand flails. Even the peeing incident.

Sabrina remembered to count the fingers and toes.

Everything was there.

Everything was perfect.

"Your baby's birthday is September ninth," the nurse continued. "And the delivery time was 1:36 p.m."

Shaw smiled, and Sabrina knew why. Their son had been born on his parents' wedding day, less than an hour after they'd said, "I Do."

"We made it," Sabrina whispered.

"We made it," Shaw whispered back. "I love you, Sabrina Tolbert."

"Good. Because I love you, too, Shaw Tolbert."

And there was no doubt in her mind about that. He was her hot cop now, and he always would be.

Shaw sneaked in another kiss and then moved back slightly so the nurse could place the baby back in Sabrina's arms. But she moved, too, maneuvering Jacob between them so that Shaw was holding him, as well.

Just like that, the baby stopped crying.

Jacob blinked. And he looked at her. His tiny forehead scrunched up, as if he might want to accuse her of something. Then, he looked at Shaw and gave him the same look before his face relaxed. He didn't smile. He just looked at them and seemed to say, "Okay, what's next?"

Shaw laughed, and Sabrina smiled through her own happy tears, which were streaming down her cheeks.

So, this was what a miracle felt like.

Now she knew.

And these miracles were hers for a lifetime.

* * * * *

Sabrina and her baby are safe,
but TEXAS MATERNITY: HOSTAGES
is just
heating up. Next month, look for
DADDY DEVASTATING
and learn more details about the aftermath,
only from Delores Fossen.
Pick it up wherever
Harlequin Intrigue books are sold!

Kay Young returned to woozy consciousness to find that she was lying on a soft sofa beneath a heap of quilts near a cheerfully burning fire. When she tried to move, however, everything hurt, and she groaned.

At once she heard a sound, then a stranger with a hard, harsh face was squatting beside her. "Shh," he said softly. "You're safe here. I promise."

"I have to go," she said weakly, struggling against pain. "He'll find me. He can't find me."

"Easy, lady," he said quietly. "You're hurt. No one's going to find you here."

"He will," she said desperately, terror clutching at her insides. "He always finds me!"

"Easy," he said again. "There's a blizzard outside. No one's getting here tonight, not even the doctor. I know, because I tried."

"Doctor? I don't need a doctor! I've got to get away."

"There's nowhere to go tonight," he said levelly. "And if I thought you could stand, I'd take you to a window and show you."

But even as she tried once more to pull away the quilts, she remembered something else: this man had been gentle when he'd found her beside the road, even when she had kicked and clawed. He hadn't hurt her.

Terror receded just a bit. She looked at him and detected signs of true concern there.

The terror eased another notch, and she let her head sag on the pillow. "He always finds me," she whispered.

"Not here. Not tonight. That much I can guarantee."

*Will Kay's mysterious rescuer protect
her from her worst fears?
Find out in HER HERO IN HIDING
by* New York Times *bestselling author
Rachel Lee.
Available June 2010,
only from Silhouette® Romantic Suspense.*

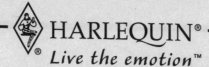

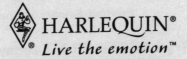

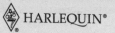

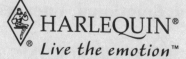

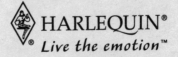

Harlequin® Historical
Historical Romantic Adventure!

*Imagine a time of chivalrous
knights and unconventional ladies,
roguish rakes and impetuous
heiresses, rugged cowboys
and spirited frontierswomen—
these rich and vivid tales will
capture your imagination!*

*Harlequin Historical . . .
they're too good to miss!*

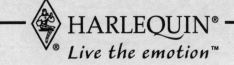

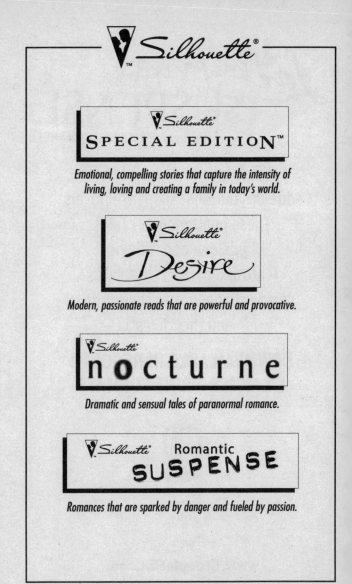

Silhouette®

Silhouette®
SPECIAL EDITION™

Emotional, compelling stories that capture the intensity of living, loving and creating a family in today's world.

Silhouette®
Desire

Modern, passionate reads that are powerful and provocative.

Silhouette®
nocturne

Dramatic and sensual tales of paranormal romance.

Silhouette® Romantic
SUSPENSE

Romances that are sparked by danger and fueled by passion.